DISNEY
Aladdin

For Jude Matthew —A. S.

DISNEY ALADDIN: FAR FROM AGRABAH
A CENTUM BOOK 978-1-913072-66-7
Published in Great Britain by Centum Books Ltd
This edition published 2019
1 3 5 7 9 10 8 6 4 2

Centum Books Ltd, 20 Devon Square, Newton Abbot, Devon, TQ12 2HR, UK
books@centumbooksltd.co.uk
CENTUM BOOKS Limited Reg. No. 07641486
A CIP catalogue record for this book is available from the British Library
Printed in United Kingdom

DISNEP
Aladdin

Far from
Agrabah

AISHA SAEED

centum

Prologue

From *LEGENDARY LEADERS ACROSS THE AGES—*
"Sultan Waleed of Sulamandra"

ONCE UPON a moonlit night in the sprawling kingdom of Sulamandra, two men squared off in a dimly lit palace room. But for their hair—the sultan's was a warm honey brown and the other's a shining silver—the two could have been mistaken for brothers. And indeed, Sultan Waleed had believed the man standing before him wearing a long green robe was a brother to him. Until now.

"Tell me it's not true," said the sultan. He held up a

cream-colored scroll. "If you tell me it's not true, I will believe you."

"I don't have the slightest idea what you're going on about," the man replied.

"Abbas, this is no time for jokes. I went against my advisor's recommendation by meeting you in private. I've even kept the guards outside to keep them from gossiping. I want to protect you, but I need your honesty. Did you send this missive to our ally? Did you ask the prince of Doran for his help in overthrowing me?"

Abbas crossed his arms and looked away. His gaze settled upon a gold-framed painting of the vast and sprawling mountains on the eastern border of Sulamandra. It hung on the wall next to an oak table, where a glass-encased lantern burned low.

"How long ago was that landscape painted?" Abbas scratched his chin. "I'd say Hasan bin Yasin was commissioned for it, based on the swirls and the color pattern. That puts it at four centuries old, doesn't it?"

"We aren't here to discuss paintings, Abbas."

"Four centuries old, that painting is," Abbas continued. "And those mountains look the same now as they ever did."

"I'm warning you . . ." the sultan said in a low voice.

"Why so flustered?" Abbas smiled. "I'm only making an observation. All that gold and silver buried and untouchable. It's a shame. A tragedy, really. And then of course there is the matter of my maps." Abbas's eyes narrowed. He glared at the oak table. "They're in that drawer, aren't they? The ones I drew up all those years ago with the precise location of every precious mineral and gem within our mountain ranges. I entrusted you with my only copy, and you've let it gather dust for over a decade."

"As I've told you before, we don't need the map, and we don't need to destroy our mountains."

"We don't require it to survive as a kingdom, but were we to extract even a tiny fraction, we would fool the gold to buy enough fleets and weapons and train enough soldiers to become the most powerful kingdom on earth."

"We are powerful and respected among all kingdoms as it is—we do not need to destroy the most fragile parts of our land for the sake of greed."

"And that is why you are a fool."

"What did you say?" The sultan's eyes widened.

"Oh, did you not hear me?" Abbas said with mock surprise. "I said that is what makes you a fool."

3

"Careful how you speak to me," the sultan warned. "We have played together since we were children. I accept your familiarity with me. But do not forget who I am."

"How can I forget?" Abbas scoffed. "You have that ridiculous emerald crown on your head, don't you?"

"Abbas." The sultan exhaled. "Our families have known each other for generations."

"They have."

"I know we have never seen eye to eye on how to develop and grow this kingdom."

"We have not."

"But despite all this, you have always been my dearest friend."

"We are not friends."

"Fine. It's true. You are more than a friend. You are like a brother to me."

"Had I been your brother, I would have been king. I'm smarter than you. I am certainly cleverer. Sulamandra could rule the entire world if you weren't so soft that you wouldn't dare harm a flower. It's time for the Akbar family name to get its full due. I deserve to be king."

"So then." The sultan's eyes brimmed with tears. "You did send the missive to Doran."

4

"Oh, yes. Not just to him, though. I sent one to every kingdom near and far. I offered a cut of Sulamandra's wealth for assistance in overthrowing you. Then I'll finally be able to use my map to make Sulamandra the wealthiest and most powerful kingdom on earth. It is a shame the prince of Doran betrayed my trust, but I'm not worried—there will be others who will send their armies to assist me. Surely some are on their way this minute."

"Abbas . . . why?"

"Because gold has a power you cannot begin to grasp."

The king stared at Abbas silently for a few moments.

"I suppose you were right, then. I was a fool, wasn't I?" the sultan finally said. "I was willing to make a million excuses for you because I loved you. I loved you so much I didn't take the veil off my eyes until now. To hear you talk this way about money and power . . . You have been given every privilege in life. Your estate rivals my own palace in size. You want for absolutely nothing and yet you are still not satisfied. I see now that your soul is hardened beyond repair; whatever good was once inside—it is long gone."

"Better a hardened soul than a weak one such as yours," Abbas scoffed.

The sultan studied Abbas for a moment and then sighed.

"You leave me no choice, then," he finally said.

The sultan turned toward the palace door.

"Oh, no." Abbas's eyes narrowed. "This is not how this story ends."

Before the sultan could take another step, Abbas lunged. The sultan stumbled. His back hit the oak table. The lantern trembled.

"What kind of sultan leaves those who would protect him outside?" Abbas laughed. He pulled out a silver knife he'd had strapped against his body and raised it in the air. "This works out far better than I'd planned, actually. Who needs an army when I can finish you off myself? Now I can say I overthrew the sultan with my own two hands. Imagine that! They'll write legends about me one day."

But as he went to attack, the sultan ducked. The knife stabbed the desk instead. Abbas grunted and yanked the weapon out, but not before the sultan's closed fist struck Abbas's jaw. Abbas crumpled against the desk. His head hit the lantern, which tumbled to the ground. The glass shattered. In an instant, the flickering flame came to life with a roar. It licked at the carpet and crawled up the ceiling, devouring centuries-old murals and paintings, turning them into ash.

And so, too, burned the oak table and the maps that lay within.

Jasmine

Chapter One

JASMINE STOOD in the palace hall holding a basket of sweet candies. She handed them out to the children standing before her now, their hands outstretched awaiting their treats. The little girls wore dresses, some with flowers, others with birds stitched upon them. The boys wore cream, brown, and sage-green tunics. One by one she plucked out candies from her basket and placed them into each child's palm—cherry, lemon, and strawberry-flavored—and the children thanked her before hurrying off happily. She watched them leave, nostalgic for her own childhood, for she had also grown up attending these festivals and had many a warm memory of eating sweets and swaying to the music without a care in the world. Those days felt many moons ago now.

The hall was aglow with lights strung against lattices; glass lanterns of pink and amber lined the walkways leading to the festivities. Jasmine smiled, pleased at the results. The Harvest Festival was one of the few things in Agrabah that fell within her domain, and she enjoyed designing the theme and look it would take on each year. The musicians, whom she had hand-selected after listening to many a questionable audition, played a lively song from their place by the dance floor. Festival attendees twirled to the music just across from where she stood. She inhaled the smell of buttery baklava and creamy pistachio pudding wafting over to her from the food stations, where renowned chefs and cooks prepared delicacies for the revelers. With the lights twinkling overhead and the music floating into the night air, as disillusioned as she'd felt lately about Agrabah—and the way her father constantly brushed her thoughts and opinions about the kingdom aside—she had to admit that when it came to the Harvest Festival, everything had worked out absolutely perfectly. If only she could push away the sadness that still lingered in her chest.

Jasmine looked around the hall yet again, scanning the room for any sign of the kind black-haired boy with the warm brown eyes. She knew it was unlikely Aladdin would have come to the festival, but still, she'd hoped. She had met him just a few days earlier when she'd traded clothes with her handmaiden and snuck out of the palace to explore the streets of Agrabah. She didn't know how he'd managed to charm her so completely, but he undeniably had. It was Aladdin who'd helped her navigate the city and truly *see* the kingdom of Agrabah as she'd always longed to. And despite the differences in their social circumstances, she and Aladdin had connected in a way she hadn't with anyone before. Jasmine remembered how, when she'd found herself lost in the city, Aladdin had held out his hand, asked her if she trusted him. Even though she'd barely known him, she had let her guard down; she *had* trusted him. But perhaps, she thought now, she'd trusted him much too easily. Because he had promised to meet her the previous night, and she'd waited well until the moon had slipped from the sky—and the boy never came. It was just as well, she supposed. What future could two people from such different worlds have? Still, the disappointment stung.

"May I have one more candy?" a little girl asked, interrupting her thoughts.

"Of course you can." Jasmine looked down at the child. She had curled pigtails tied in ribbons and grinned as Jasmine handed her a maple-flavored sweet. The girl thanked the princess before hurrying off. Jasmine watched as she looped around one of the hall's bronze pillars, passed a group of boys in starched tunics tossing a ball back and forth, and finally joined her mother, who stood in line for grilled kebabs and a cheese pastry the chef was preparing warm and fresh. The mother looked down and smiled at her daughter. Jasmine remembered her own mother smiling at her the same way. The Queen had been a great leader and had infused in Jasmine her love for learning and her passion for leadership. Had her mother still been alive, Jasmine's life would have turned out quite differently. Even when Jasmine was a child, her mother had taken her desire to be sultana seriously— indeed, she had been preparing Jasmine for that very role until her untimely and tragic death changed everything.

From the corner of her eye, Jasmine noticed Prince Anders. It was hard to miss him, what with his fuchsia and green royal costume and the ridiculous fur-lined hat he never took off, even in the balmy heat of Agrabah. Right now, he positively glowed from the praise and adulation of the people surrounding him. Which was just as well—their attention kept him from regaling *her* with tales of his lands and his brilliance. In contrast to Prince Anders, the other visiting royal, Prince Ali of Ababwa (a kingdom so obscure even *she* hadn't heard of it) seemed to be keeping to himself. He stood awkwardly against the wall opposite her. While Prince Anders's outfit was completely over the top, Prince Ali wore a gold-fringed cream outfit that was simple enough, even if the costume involved so many layers it looked as though his clothing intended to swallow him whole. Still, he was dressed far more plainly than she'd have expected of someone who'd barreled into town with the most obnoxious entourage she'd ever seen, replete with marching drummers, dancers, peacocks, and golden camels. He had arrived standing on a flower-covered *camel float*, of all things. And yet now he stood on the other side of the room, staring at his surroundings as though he'd never been inside a palace before.

"He seems different." It was Dalia, Jasmine's hand-maiden and best friend, who spoke, nodding toward Prince Ali. "And his friend is incredibly attractive, so please make it work?"

Jasmine glanced at the jovial-looking advisor standing next to the prince; he was broad-shouldered, wore blue, and stood a bit taller than Ali.

"What about the prince?" Jasmine raised an eyebrow.

"Seems cute in a nervous, low-self-esteem kind of way." Dalia shrugged. "He's trying too hard."

"That's the problem," Jasmine said. "I need someone with more heart." She glanced at Ali and suddenly felt bad for her harsh words. It wasn't *his* fault he'd come courting—her father was obsessed with marriage and constantly encouraged princely suitors when all Jasmine wanted was a seat at the table to help lead Agrabah in the right direction for the sake of its people. Ali didn't know marriage was the last thing on her mind. As far as princes went, though, she had to admit he didn't seem quite as bad as the others who'd come to try to win her hand. Sure, what with his poor attempts at smooth talking, he'd put his foot in his mouth more times than she could count in the brief exchanges they'd had since he'd arrived at the palace. But even if his execution was awkward, his intentions were good—she could tell that much.

"Here he comes! He's coming!" Dalia's eyes widened. "Act natural."

Jasmine suppressed a smile as Prince Ali approached.

"Sorry for earlier," he told her. "I didn't mean to . . . I'm not used to partying. I mean, I am, but . . ."

Dalia was right, Jasmine thought. Despite herself, she smiled at him. He *was* kind of adorable—in a nervous sort of way.

"Dance?" Jasmine interrupted him. She needed to put him out of his misery. "I'd love to."

Prince Ali's eyes widened, but before he could say anything else, she led him to the dance floor. Music swelled around them as the musicians began their next song. Jasmine began to move to the beat, but Ali's feet looked permanently glued to the ground. *Now what's the matter?* she wondered. She was about to ask him if he was all right when suddenly he began dancing—if one could call it that. His hands and legs flailed about him as though he were a puppet. *What on earth . . . ?* thought

Jasmine. But she smiled in spite of herself. He was trying. She'd give him that much.

Seeing the shift in her expression, Ali grinned. It was the first genuine smile she'd seen from him since they'd met, and as she noticed the way his dimple deepened, something inside her softened. When the next song began, Ali swept Jasmine into his arms. Once his nerves had settled, it turned out he was actually a good dancer. A *very* good dancer. And there was something about those eyes—they looked familiar somehow. Comforting. With his arms around her waist, they moved across the dance floor. Looking into his deep brown eyes, she felt as though the crowd had melted away and it was just the two of them in all the world.

She gazed at Prince Ali. Who *was* this mysterious prince? What was his story?

The music shifted then, pulling both of them out of their reveries. The next song was a popular one and more up-tempo. Prince Ali's eyes lit up. Pulling her back, he spun her out across the dance floor. And then—he danced. Without her. Jasmine watched from the side-lines. He danced like his feet were on fire. He pivoted and spun, and soon a crowd of attendees surrounded him on the dance floor, clapping and cheering him on as they swayed to the music.

Jasmine's heart sank. Just like that, the moment was over.

When the music stopped, Prince Ali looked through the crowd until his eyes landed on hers. There it was. That self-satisfied, smug grin. Just like Prince Anders's. He had managed to charm her with one dance, and she'd let her loneliness get the best of her, believing there was more to him than there was. But there wasn't more to him. There was no mystery. He was a wealthy, attention-seeking prince, just like all the others before him.

Suddenly, Jasmine felt weary. She was tired of compromising and making the best of her stifling situation. She was tired of men appearing at her doorstep day after day, looking at her as an object of conquest. Why had she even bothered to come to this at all? She'd have been better off staying in her quarters finishing up with rereading *Legendary Leaders Across the Ages*. There was nothing at this festival—or in Agrabah—for her.

Without another word, Jasmine swallowed her disappointment, turned on her heel, and walked away.

Aladdin

Chapter Two

*A*LADDIN WATCHED the flickering glow of the lanterns in the courtyard below as he stood on the edge of Jasmine's balcony. The music from the Harvest Festival played faintly beneath him. Palm trees rustled against one another. The moon glowed full and bright against the night sky, the stars a glittering blanket above.

He half expected Abu to scamper up one of the trees. It felt strange not to have his pet monkey by his side. But Jasmine had met Abu when they'd explored Agrabah together—seeing him here now would have given the whole thing away. And he knew Abu was enjoying being pampered in Aladdin's guest quarters anyway.

Aladdin plucked a wayward silk thread from his royal outfit. He'd wished to be a prince, and Genie had done a perfect job in granting his wish. The clothing still felt strange, though, with all its poufy layers. The hat itched a bit, too. He fidgeted. Regardless of what he thought about his clothing, none of it mattered if he couldn't erase the look of disappointment that had settled across Jasmine's face earlier that evening.

The three wishes Genie had granted Aladdin when he'd rubbed the golden lamp had initially seemed like plenty. But Aladdin had already used up his first wish to become prince of the fictional "Ababwa," and he'd promised his last wish to Genie to free his friend from a lifetime of servitude, which left Aladdin with only one. And since he couldn't wish for more wishes—Genie had been *quite* clear about that—he needed to make each of them count.

The magic carpet hovered on the other side of the balcony, just out of sight. Aladdin glanced down at it now; it waggled a tassel in greeting.

"Shouldn't be long," Aladdin promised.

Jasmine's room was still empty. As Aladdin studied the red roses climbing up the pillars across from him and the golden goblets of carefully arranged flowers along the balcony, doubt crept into his mind. Genie was distracting Jasmine's handmaiden right this minute, inviting her for a stroll through the palace grounds so Aladdin could have a chance to smooth things over with Jasmine. But was it really the best idea to sneak into Jasmine's quarters like this? His palms began to sweat, panic rising. He'd need to think fast about exactly what to say before she called out for every armed guard in the palace to arrest him at once. And if she did, who could blame her?

It had all been going so well at the Harvest Festival. She'd forgiven him for his awkwardness when he'd first arrived at the palace. And then later, when they danced together they connected, just like they had when they'd met on the streets of Agrabah. She was beginning to like him; at least, she seemed to be. When his favorite song had begun to play, he'd thought he'd finally found his opportunity to *really* impress the princess. And while the crowd of people around him had cheered, he'd watched as disappointment spread across Jasmine's face. He realized then what he must have looked like to her—just another prince, there for the attention and praise. She didn't realize he was only there for her.

Aladdin had never connected with anyone the way he had with Jasmine that day on the streets of Agrabah. And when he'd discovered she was not a handmaiden of the palace but the princess herself, Aladdin felt heartbroken. As a street rat, he could never have a chance with a princess. But now, thanks to Genie, he was Prince Ali—worthy of trying to win her heart.

Suddenly, he stood up straighter. There was Jasmine. Just across from where he stood. She walked toward a collection of papers spread across a large desk. She was so engrossed in them she didn't notice him standing there. Yet. Aladdin took a deep breath. He needed to get this right. He had to. This was his last chance to smooth things over. Whatever he said, it needed to work.

You can do it, Aladdin told himself.

But could he?

He tapped his knuckles against the balcony to get her attention, but she was so immersed in what Aladdin could now make out was an array of maps that she didn't notice him. He hesitated before knocking louder.

"Come in," Jasmine said without glancing up.

"I'm in already," said Aladdin.

Jasmine looked up with a start; her eyes widened. And then they narrowed.

From seemingly out of nowhere, a tiger popped into view. And while Aladdin had never actually met a tiger before, this one seemed particularly enormous. Its fur shone a brilliant orange with white and black stripes across its body. The tiger faced him. And then, baring its teeth, it snarled at Aladdin.

Jasmine quickly stood and held up a hand toward Aladdin.

"Don't move!" she warned.

"I won't." Aladdin raised his hands in the air. "I came because you left so abruptly."

"How did you get here?"

"Magic carpet."

"Huh." She raised an eyebrow. "Actually, now that you're here, I can't seem to find Ababwa on any of my maps. Can you show me?"

"Am I allowed to move?" Aladdin glanced at the tiger. "Nice kitty?" The tiger growled, baring its teeth wider.

"Raja, don't eat the prince," Jasmine said. "He needs his legs for dancing."

Aladdin flushed. "Did I go too far?"

"A little." She nodded. "So . . . Ababwa."

Aladdin edged past the tiger, which still studied him suspiciously, and picked up a map. This was going to be fun—showing her a country that did not actually exist. She didn't seem too upset about the dance floor debacle, but now he'd gone and made things much worse. He had to find Ababwa on a map or be exposed as a fraud—which, Aladdin supposed, swallowing nervously, he was. How on earth would he get out of this one? He lifted the map up, obscuring himself from Jasmine's view.

"Genie," Aladdin whispered under his breath from behind the map, hoping the powerful being could hear him. "She has a lot of maps. I need to find Ababwa."

"Have you lost your country?" Jasmine asked sweetly.

"No, no, of course not," Aladdin said quickly just as Genie showed up on the map, so small he was almost imperceptible. He jumped up and down, pointing to where letters began to appear, spelling out the word *Ababwa*.

"Thanks," Aladdin whispered. He could've kissed his

little blue friend. Giddy with relief, he lowered the map. "See?" He pointed. "There it is."

Jasmine leaned down to look at it.

"I don't think so." She frowned as she studied the map. "No, it's not . . ." But there was no denying it. There it was: THE KINGDOM OF ABABWA. She looked at another map to check its accuracy. Aladdin glanced around. There were so many maps of all different sizes. Many of them were marked, most of them worn around the edges. But they all now seemed to display the fictional kingdom of Ababwa, clear as day.

"How did I not see that?" Jasmine wondered.

"Maps are old and useless. No practical value." Aladdin shrugged, trying his best to move away from the topic.

"Maps are how I see the world."

"Really? I'd think a princess could go anywhere."

"Not this princess."

Aladdin brightened. He had the perfect way to make things up to Jasmine! And it was waiting for them just a few feet away.

"Well . . ." Aladdin leaned against a pillar as casually as he could muster, brushing some dust off his shoulder. "Would you want to—" But before he could finish his sentence, the pillar wobbled. A bowl of red pomegranates crashed to the ground.

So this plan is going great. Aladdin sighed. He bent down to pick up the pomegranates and put them back in their bowl. Raja walked up and licked his face. It must be going really poorly if the tiger was feeling sorry for him.

"Thanks," Aladdin said. "I needed a face wash."

Raja nuzzled Aladdin and purred. Aladdin petted the tiger and rubbed its ears. Cats loved getting their ears rubbed, at least the ones in Agrabah did, and wasn't a tiger basically an overgrown cat? He looked up at Jasmine; she was staring at the two of them like they were doing synchronized cartwheels together.

"So, I was saying," Aladdin said, straightening. "We should go see these places. There's a whole world outside of books . . . Do you want to?"

"With you?"

"Yes."

"How? All the doors are guarded."

"Who said anything about doors? Sometimes, Princess," Aladdin said, "you just need to take a risk."

He walked toward the balcony. This was it. His moment

to make up for all the mistakes from this evening. If this didn't work, nothing would. He leapt up to the balcony railing and stepped off the edge—out of sight.

"What are you doing?" Jasmine gasped and rushed toward the balcony. "What just happened?"

Slowly, Aladdin floated back up. Jasmine's mouth fell open as she took in the sight of him upon the magic carpet.

"What is that?" she asked, her voice hushed.

"My magic carpet. I told you." He held out his hand toward her. "Do you trust me?"

"What did you say?" Jasmine looked at him now in the most peculiar way.

"Do you trust me?"

She studied the carpet. Had he said the wrong thing? he wondered. A million questions played upon her lips. She reached her hand toward him, but then she hesitated. Aladdin tried to stay calm. She had to take his hand. She had to. If she didn't . . .

But she did.

She took his hand.

She nimbly climbed upon the magic carpet, sitting next to him.

Before either of them could say another word, it whisked them into the air.

Aladdin looked up at the stars. The night sky was dark and lovely.

It was filled with possibilities.

Jasmine

Chapter Three

JASMINE COULDN'T believe it. More surprising than the magic carpet flying straight into the sky was the fact that she'd taken Ali's outstretched hand. She was not the sort to get swept away—to trust a complete stranger this easily—but there was just something about him. Maybe it was the way he looked at her, the sweet boyish look of hope in his eyes. Or maybe it was what he had said: *Do you trust me?* Those four words. The same words Aladdin had said to her on the streets of Agrabah. And she had trusted

Aladdin, just as she now trusted Prince Ali. What was happening to her? After a lifetime of cynicism, was she going . . . soft? She wasn't sure. She *did* know that against all odds, right this minute, she was soaring into the sky, the clouds around her, sitting next to a prince she'd just met earlier that afternoon.

"You okay?" Prince Ali nudged her gently. "Not carpet-sick, are you? That's actually a thing, you know."

"No," she said. "I mean, I—whoa!" A gust of wind rushed against them. Ali placed an arm around her; Jasmine gripped the rug tightly as it swayed. The magic carpet fluttered, then readjusted, rising farther into the sky.

"Sorry," Ali apologized as the rug straightened out and the air returned to a gentle breeze. "The wind can get unpredictable when we're still climbing up, but it should settle now. And don't worry about falling—the magic carpet is really sturdy." She glanced at his arm, still around her shoulder. "Oh!" His eyes widened. He pulled away. "I didn't mean to make you uncomfortable. I just . . . the rug slipped, and . . ."

"No, it's fine. I appreciated the reassurance." Jasmine looked down at the rug beneath them. "You're right about this carpet, though. I never thought one could actually fly, much less be this sturdy."

"There is definitely more to it than meets the eye," he told her. "Now tell me, Princess, where would you like to go?"

"Where *can* we go?"

"Anywhere you'd like."

"Anywhere? There's a whole world out there to see."

"Whole world? You got it!"

Jasmine laughed. "We don't have time for that."

"You'd be surprised. Magic carpets make good time." Ali's eyes twinkled. "Hold on tight!"

The clear sky above and the deep dark ocean below blurred into one another as the magic carpet geared up. Before Jasmine could ask any more questions, they zipped further into the night sky. Trepidation filled Jasmine's mind. Where were they going? Sure, Ali seemed comfortable on this rug, but was this honestly safe? She braced herself and shut her eyes. In a matter of seconds, the magic carpet stopped. Opening her eyes, Jasmine blinked.

"Is that . . . is that *snow*?" she asked in disbelief.

Indeed, far below them was a wide-open meadow, dotted with yellow flowers and snowy patches of ice, overlooking a crystal-clear lake. She was about to ask him just how far from home the magic carpet had taken them when her gaze shifted upward. Red, green, and purple lights streaked across the night sky.

"That's the aurora borealis," she whispered, scarcely believing it. "I've only read about it in books."

"Nicer in person?"

"There's no comparison . . ." she said with awe. "But how did we get here so fast? How can this be real?"

"Magic," Ali said simply.

They lingered for a bit, watching the sky light up in all its brilliant spectacle before the magic carpet blurred the landscape once more and whisked them over thundering waterfalls, misty jungles, and wide-open savannahs. They watched monkeys swing from branch to branch through shady canopies and listened to the howl of hyenas as they galloped below. And then the magic carpet rumbled again, and within seconds Jasmine and Ali stood atop a pristine mountain peak. Their feet sank into the cool snow. The world was dark and silent below them.

"There are no other footsteps here." Jasmine glanced at the ground. "Not even animal tracks."

"Well, this definitely looks like the highest peak." Ali

looked around. "Maybe we're the first to have reached the summit. Think about it . . ." His eyes glinted with a smile. "You and I are discovering new lands together."

"Probably not." Jasmine laughed, thinking about her detailed maps and books about geography. But it was a nice thought. She wondered who ruled the land below them. Had she been sultana, she might have visited this country on diplomatic missions and seen these very mountain peaks from a different perspective. Well, she reminded herself, at least she was here now.

Back on the carpet, they sailed gently now, cresting over wind gusts and looking down at twinkling city lights below them. Dalia was never going to believe any of this.

"This is exactly what I needed," Jasmine told Ali as the carpet floated along. "Sometimes life can start to fall into a rut. You know how it is, I'm sure. You do the same thing every single day and then you see this whole new world and realize . . ."

"How beautiful our world is."

"Exactly. I mean, even if we took this magic carpet and flew to every place on earth, we'd still end up missing *something*." She turned to look at him. "Thank you so much for this adventure. I know I won't forget any of it."

And I won't forget that I got to see it all with you, she thought as she studied his profile. Jasmine knew that, as a prince, Ali must have traveled the world three or four times over, and with a magic carpet for a friend surely none of what they'd seen was new to him. Yet he seemed just as excited and awestruck as she felt. He hadn't grown jaded like the other princes she had met over the years; he, too, was genuinely in love with the world. She liked to think that if she had the chance to travel and explore the world on diplomatic missions for Agrabah, she, too, would retain her sense of gratitude for the beauty of the world around them.

Ali's eyes met hers. Looking at him now, she felt herself go off-kilter. Those eyes were liquid brown and so deep—she could get lost in them.

No.

She couldn't fall for him. She did not have time for that. She cleared her throat and looked away. Peering over the edge of the magic carpet, she noticed a tiny patch of land beneath them.

"Is that an island?" She pointed down below. "Must be the smallest one we've flown over so far."

"Hard to make it out." Ali leaned over and squinted. "Even with all the moonlight."

"It's so dark, it must be uninhabited."

The carpet, intuitive as ever, swept down gently so they could get a better look.

"Wait . . ." Ali's voice trailed off. "There *is* some light. It's not coming from the island, though—it's surrounding it."

He was right. The lower the magic carpet floated, the clearer they saw a thin band of light that ringed the island.

"Maybe it's the moon's reflection?"

"Maybe," Jasmine mused. "But it looks like the water is glowing. Could it be electric eels? Or bioluminescent fish? I've read about them . . . Do you think we could go down there? Unless you're tired, of course. It *has* been a long night."

"Your wish is my command, Princess."

"And we won't get too delayed?" she asked, the concern suddenly—not to mention annoyingly—springing to mind. "I don't know what my father would do if he discovered I was missing."

"Don't worry," he reassured her. "Part of the magic of flying by carpet is both seeing the world and experiencing time in ways we can't fully understand." He patted the carpet gently. "Can you take us down, buddy? Just want to explore one last thing."

The magic carpet nodded a tassel in assent and slowly began its descent to the island below.

Jasmine wasn't sure she understood how time could slow down or work differently when traveling by magic carpet, but until tonight she hadn't known a magic carpet ride was possible in the first place. He had asked her if she trusted him, and tonight, perhaps she would. She wanted to see the island and what the glowing ring of light was all about, it was true. But a part of her was also grateful for this interlude because she simply didn't want the night to end.

Aladdin

Chapter Four

ALADDIN WANTED to pinch himself to make sure this wasn't all just a dream. Was he really on a magic carpet ride with Princess Jasmine? Exploring glacier lakes and soaring past waterfalls? He couldn't wait to tell Abu all about the cheetahs prowling in the tall grass and the silverback gorillas that had watched their flight under the moonlit sky. Their time together was going better than he could have imagined, but—not for the first time—Aladdin wondered what would happen once they returned. Sooner or later she'd find out he was not actually a prince but just another commoner from the streets of Agrabah. Would she be furious? Would the doors to her heart be shut to him forever? He simmered at the injustice of it all. To connect with someone but not be worthy of them because of one's station in life. Aladdin sighed. This wasn't the time to dwell on that. There would be time to sort through all of that later; for now, he wanted to enjoy his time with Jasmine.

The carpet descended onto the small island. It was a lush parcel of land with palm trees and bushes that bloomed with pink, red, and orange flowers. Touching down now, he saw the water glowed a blend of yellow and sparkling green.

The magic carpet hovered just close enough to the ground to allow them to step off easily onto the sandy shore.

"I resent that, you know." Aladdin wagged a finger at the carpet. "The landings are always bumpy when it's just me, and *now* you're so careful. I think I know why."

The carpet raised a tassel and shrugged.

Aladdin laughed, but he agreed; Jasmine was worth taking extra care for.

"Thanks." Jasmine petted the carpet. As much as the magic carpet had taken to Jasmine, it was undeniable that Jasmine had grown equally fond of it as well.

"The color is much deeper now that we're at eye level," Jasmine said as they walked to the edge of the shore. They bent down to examine the ocean. The water glowed as though sparkling jewels lay buried below. But they weren't jewels. They were the fish Jasmine had suspected. "They *are* bioluminescent," she said.

"So many of them," Aladdin said. He watched them flit back and forth. Their rapid movement seemed to be what lent the fuzzy glow of light to the water. Their colors looked all the more incredible juxtaposed as they were against the dark ocean stretching into the horizon. Jasmine and Aladdin watched for a while in silence before trailing the island's edge, taking in the tropical scenery around them. Palm trees flanked the perimeter of the island's beach. Their trunks were copper colored, and their bright green leaves swayed in the gentle ocean breeze. The sand was white as pearls and so soft their feet sank right in.

Just then, Aladdin heard a dull thud in the distance. He tensed. "Did you hear that?"

"I did," Jasmine whispered. "It came from behind us."

The carpet followed closely as the pair tentatively edged toward the source of the noise. Aladdin was grateful for his magical friend by their side, ready to sweep them away in an instant if needed. The wind rustled as they slipped between the palm trees. A small pond shimmered steps away. Just then, a strong gust whipped through the leaves and three brown coconuts knocked loudly against a tree trunk before tumbling to the ground and rolling next to Aladdin's feet.

"Coconuts." Aladdin kneeled down and picked one up. "Glad I was at the ready to protect you from these dangerous beasts."

"They're louder than you'd think with this place being so quiet." Jasmine smiled. She walked over to the pond, kicked off her shoes, and dipped a toe in. "It's warm! There may be a volcano nearby—funny, I didn't see any sign of one when we were flying. You'd at least see some lava sparks or smoke on the horizon . . . at least I thought so. Wouldn't have even known one could be close to us were it not for this little patch of water."

"How do you know so many things?" Aladdin rolled his pants up and sat next to her. The water lapped against his ankles. "Everywhere we've traveled, you knew *something* about it. Even here, on this quiet little island."

"Books," she answered.

"Got to get me one of those." He grinned.

They sat together in companionable silence for a moment, their feet dipped in the warm salt water, the palm trees swaying and rustling around them.

After a moment, Jasmine spoke. "I've loved everything we've seen tonight, but I have to admit that this is the best part of the trip so far."

"Mine too. Good call to take a detour to this island."

"I've been known to make some good calls now and then."

"I agree. Your decision to take that carpet ride with me was a fine example of your excellent judgment."

"Yes." She met his gaze. "It most certainly was."

Strands of stray hair swept across Jasmine's forehead. With the moonlight shining down upon her, she looked so lovely and—there it was again. Aladdin felt that familiar pang of guilt as he saw that her eyes were filled with trust. In *him*. And he couldn't tell her who he was. Not yet, anyway.

Suddenly, Jasmine's eyes brightened.

"I just realized something!" she said. "I'm a little turned around on my geography right now, but I think we shouldn't be too far away from Ababwa based on its coordinates on the maps I looked at."

"Oh . . ." Aladdin's eyes widened. "No, I think we're pretty far away."

"But even then, with the carpet it won't take any time at all to get there, right?"

"Well . . ."

"I mean, if it could take us past a tropical waterfall and then over to a snowy mountain peak in a matter of seconds, it should be able to take us to Ababwa for a quick little visit."

The carpet perked up its tassel at this and followed the conversation earnestly. In this moment Aladdin was grateful the magic rug didn't have a face. He was pretty sure its amused expression would have given everything away.

"I didn't mean to be pushy," Jasmine said apologetically. "I guess I thought it would be nice. You've seen where I'm from. It might be great to see where you came from. What makes you tick."

"Yeah, that makes sense," Aladdin said slowly. If there had been a kingdom to take her to, he'd have done so in an instant. But where could he take her? And how could he say no to her without ending their time together on a note of disappointment? He knew she would find him out eventually; he just hadn't realized it would be on this very trip.

A low-throated moan rendered them both still.

"Now *that* wasn't a coconut," Jasmine whispered.

Aladdin grabbed Jasmine's hand, and in an instant, they leapt atop the carpet, leaving their shoes behind. Flying above the tree line, they searched for the source of the noise.

"A whale!" Jasmine gasped and pointed toward the ocean.

There it was, plain as the moonlight above. An enormous gray whale floated in the dark waters ahead, not far from the shore—and beside it, a family of dolphins splashed and somersaulted in the water.

"I'd read about them, but I had no idea they sounded like that. And look! Next to them! Pink dolphins." She pointed. "There are only a handful of them left in the world."

The carpet lowered Jasmine and Aladdin to the island's sandy shore, where they all stared at the beautiful creatures. Then the carpet dusted sand off its tassels and darted toward the water.

"Careful! Not so fast," Jasmine called out. "We don't want to scare them away!"

"Oh, the carpet is a favorite with animals. All sorts," Aladdin reassured her.

"Want to walk over and maybe wade into the water a bit to get a closer look?" she asked him.

"Sure. Um, let me just get our shoes from the pond so we have them."

"Well, hurry before they head off," Jasmine said. "I'll go keep an eye on the carpet."

Aladdin watched her walk toward the shoreline before he slipped through the palm trees. Once the dolphins went on their way and Jasmine returned, so too would her question. There was no denying that if the magic carpet could zip through jungles and take them atop snowy Alps in a matter of moments, it could certainly have taken them for a visit to Ababwa. He tried out different excuses—the kingdom was closed for renovations? Fumigation? There was an important confidential meeting underway they couldn't interrupt? He raced to think of something—anything—he could say that would sound believable, but nothing worked.

"Would be great if you were here, Genie." He sighed. "I could really use your help."

The tap on his shoulder just then nearly made him jump out of his skin.

"Genie!" Aladdin exclaimed. He glanced back at Jasmine, but she had waded up to her knees to pet a dolphin that had swum close to the shore. "What are you doing here?"

"You called me. I came. That's how it works, you know. Genie at your service." The blue genie curtsied and grinned. "Been wondering where you were." He looked around. "This is quite the romantic spot. Nicely done, my friend. Color me impressed!"

"Uh, thanks."

"So, what can I do you for?" Genie asked. "Mind you, I can't be gone too long. Got a serious job with distracting the people who would pick up on the fact that you two are missing. It's a tough job, but someone's got to do it." He winked.

"Get over here." Aladdin hurried toward a thick patch

of palm trees and ducked behind them. He glanced back at the shoreline, but neither Jasmine nor the carpet had noticed a thing.

For now.

"So, tell me everything," Genie said. "Things going well? Has she warmed up to you? Need some romantic tips? Can't make someone fall in love with you, but can definitely give you advice. I got a drawer full of tips. The biggest thing is not to appear too pathetic. It's an adorable look on a puppy, not so much if you're trying to win the heart of a princess. Trust me on that, kid."

"No, it's not that. Jasmine and I have been getting along well. Great, actually. But then she started talking about how we'd seen so many fantastic sights but hadn't seen the one place she really wanted to see, and if we could just . . ."

"She asked to visit Ababwa, didn't she?"

"How'd you know?"

"I could've seen that coming from a mile away, kid." Genie shook his head. "It's a fair question on her part, though, isn't it?"

"I know, but how do I take her somewhere that doesn't exist?"

"Poor Al." Genie shook his head. "You've gotten yourself into quite the pickle, haven't you?"

Aladdin looked down at the sand. He felt embarrassed. Genie was right. It should have been obvious from the beginning of their adventure that Jasmine would ask to visit his imaginary kingdom. How could he not have planned for that?

But then—Aladdin's eyes widened as he realized something else. He turned to Genie.

"Actually, it's not a pickle at all." A slow smile spread across Aladdin's face. "Because Ababwa can be real. *You* can make Ababwa happen. I mean, you were able to make that parade with all the elephants and guards and dancers and drums and camels. You whipped all that up out of nothing! You could make a kingdom for me, couldn't you?"

"Of course I can." Genie nodded. "Heck, I could make you ten kingdoms. Architecture is a pet hobby of mine, actually. It would be my absolute pleasure to design you the kingdom of your dreams."

"Okay, great," Aladdin said. "Let's do it!"

"Sure thing." Genie cracked his knuckles and magically produced the lamp.

They both looked at each other with eyebrows raised expectantly.

"Well, go on, then," Genie finally said. "I haven't got all day."

"What do you mean?" Aladdin smiled.

"Seriously, kid, I don't have time for this," huffed Genie. "I have to get back to the handmaiden. She needs, um, distracting, as you know, and she's really good company, I must admit. So go on and make your wish and I'll make you the nicest and grandest kingdom you've ever dreamed of. Just say the magic words."

"But that's the thing, Genie. I don't have to use a wish for this."

"Oh yeah?" Genie cocked his head. "How do you figure?"

"Because this isn't a new wish. It's part of the first one. When you made me a prince, you made me prince of a place called Ababwa. So you have to make the place I'm the prince of, don't you? That's pretty much implied in the whole shebang of making me royalty, isn't it?"

Genie's smile froze. Then his jaw dropped.

"No. That can't be right." He frowned. "I mean, when I said I'd make you a prince, I . . ." Genie sighed and massaged his temples. "Or I guess it is right," he said reluctantly. "You're good, kid. I'll give you that much. Annoying at times, but definitely good. So, let me see." He rested his back against a palm tree. The tree trembled and a coconut rustled and tumbled to the ground next to his feet. Genie picked it up, popped in a straw, and took a sip.

"Making a kingdom isn't going to be hard. Placing it exactly where it showed up on the map, though, that's tricky. We can probably work around that since the magic carpet flies too fast to keep track of location. But we can't have people already living there since they'll wonder why a new nation popped up out of nowhere. Folks tend to notice and ask questions about that kind of thing. But then it has to be big enough to actually look realistic." Genie took another sip of the coconut juice, and then his eyes brightened.

"That's it!" He snapped his fingers. "Moribania!" Why didn't I think about that first?"

"Moribania?"

"Well, it *was* the kingdom of Moribania," said Genie. "They relocated not too long ago after an earthquake turned it into rubble. It's abandoned, virtually deserted now." Genie frowned and concentrated. "It's far from here, but with the carpet, distance doesn't matter anyway. Yep, I think that could work."

"I don't mean to disparage your skills or anything," Aladdin said. "I mean, the dancers and the whole entourage in Agrabah were really impressive. But this is a whole kingdom we're talking about. A palace and a village square, boats for a dock and all that. The land won't be too much work for you, will it?"

Genie puffed up at this. "Honestly, Al. If I were a lesser genie, my ego would be royally hurt at you questioning my expertise." He snapped his fingers and a pencil appeared behind his ear. He whipped out a scroll of blueprints from thin air and opened them wide. They floated before him, and with a ruler and pencil, Genie began to draw and jot down notes.

"So, tell me, kid," he said. His pencil balanced in his teeth. "If you could have the perfect kingdom—which you will, when I'm done with it—what would it look like?"

"The perfect kingdom?" Aladdin asked.

"Yep." Genie nodded. "I mean, keep in mind she's going to have to buy that it's real, so stay a little grounded with your choices. But otherwise, yes, dream big, kid."

"Well, it would have to be magnificent," Aladdin said. "Bustling and busy with lots of people, but not so busy that it's overcrowded and overwhelming like it can get in Agrabah." Genie kept his eyes on the paper and took notes, nodding along as Aladdin spoke. "And the palace should be really nice. I'm talking minarets that graze the clouds. Lots of grand staircases. A huge foyer! Fifty bedrooms, give or take a few. Jasmine is used to royal setups, so this one has to stand out and be fancy enough for her to really pause and take notice."

"Super fancy." Genie nodded. "Got it."

"A courtyard would be good, too." Aladdin paused. "My mother loved the courtyards of Agrabah. She'd tell me stories about the house we'd have someday with a courtyard of pastel pots and the plants we'd grow in them. It was our favorite thing to daydream about together. That part doesn't need to be fancy. Just nice and tasteful. Oh!" Aladdin raised his eyebrows. "It should also have a pretty fantastic menagerie. It might be nice for her to see animals and birds she's never seen before. Some uniquely sculpted gardens on the palace grounds would also be great. The town itself should be charming with cobblestone walkways and a quaint little square. Maybe a lagoon that looks like this one tucked away somewhere? Meadows and cliffs. And interesting shops."

"What sort of shops?"

"A café, for starters. Like the one back home—you know, Bilal's Teas and Sweets?"

"That old hole in the wall?" Genie wrinkled his nose.

"Yeah, it's not much to look at, but his desserts are better than anything in the world," Aladdin said. "Of course, in Ababwa, the shop would have a fresh coat of paint and chairs that didn't wobble. Oh, and a map store! Jasmine would love that!"

"Got it. Anything else?"

"I guess I just want Ababwa to be the kind of place where people get along. It should be safe and clean and perfect."

Genie cleared his throat and looked up from his blue-prints.

"I'm not sure it can be absolutely perfect," he reminded Aladdin. "I mean, it would make her suspicious if it looked like a land out of a fairy tale, wouldn't it? No matter where you go, there are always issues."

"Maybe you're right," Aladdin conceded. "I want it

to be as good as it can be, then. And if there have to be problems in my kingdom, I want to be the kind of royal who will try to help fix those problems." He shook his head, realizing he'd gotten caught up in the fantasy of it all. "What do you think?" he asked a little self-consciously.

"That sounds nice, kid." Genie smiled. "Sure, Al, I can do all that. And for what it's worth, I think you'd make a fine prince." Genie jotted down some more notes before he closed his eyes and rested a hand atop Aladdin's head.

"What are you doing?" Aladdin asked.

"Checking out your memories for a little inspiration." He rested his hand for a few more moments and mumbled some words under his breath, and then—"Voilà!" He lifted his hand from Aladdin's head and opened his eyes. "There it is!" He snapped his finger and then folded his arms.

"There's what?"

"Well, not here." Genie rolled his eyes. "You're very literal, you know that? The kingdom. Your kingdom of Ababwa. It's done. A whole brand-spanking-new kingdom for you to rule. I've got to say, I've really outdone myself this time. You'll love it. Just fly over the country up ahead, take a left at the string of islands and atolls, and bam! You won't miss it, what with the towering minarets you asked for."

"That sounds amazing! Thank you so much, Genie," Aladdin said.

"Amazing is what I do." Genie grinned.

"And it will look completely real?"

"As real as you and me. Won't be able to tell the difference."

"How long will it *stay* a real kingdom?"

"Don't worry," Genie reassured him. "I've designed it so that it'll be around as long as you both are there."

"So, we can stay a few hours?"

"Longer if you want. Time will work differently while you're there. Feel free to take as long as you'd like. When you're ready to fly away, Ababwa will vanish and go back to how it was before."

"I don't know how to begin to thank you. I really appreciate it."

Just then, they were interrupted by the sound of Jasmine's voice.

"Ali?"

Aladdin nearly yelped. Turning, he spotted her approaching him from the other side of the palm trees. He swallowed. How could he begin to explain away the big blue man standing just on the other side of him?

"Oh, I can explain," Aladdin began.

"Took me a minute to find where you'd gone off to. Who were you talking to?"

He met her gaze but then realized she wasn't looking at Genie. She was looking at something on his shoulder.

"Is that a spider?" she asked.

Aladdin blinked. Sure enough, there was no blue man anywhere in sight. Instead, a big black glittering spider was perched on Aladdin's shoulder like a parrot.

"I heard you talking just now. You appreciate . . . the spider?"

The spider raised one black spindly leg and waved.

"Um, yes," Aladdin said, improvising. "This is Bitsy. My . . . um . . . pet spider. He was flying right behind us, hanging from a tassel like he always does. A bit of a daredevil."

"I didn't notice him before."

"No? Well, he likes to keep to himself."

Jasmine raised an eyebrow and stared at Aladdin.

"You have a pet spider. Really? You know those big black ones can be dangerous, right?"

"Well, you have a pet tiger," Aladdin countered. "Heard those can be a bit temperamental as well, can't they?"

"That's not the same at all. . . ." Jasmine shook her head, but then she laughed. "Okay, fair point."

"So," Aladdin said. "About Ababwa."

"Yes?" Her eyes lit up.

"Let's go."

From *LEGENDARY LEADERS
ACROSS THE AGES—*
"Zayn the Tenth, or:
How Kindness Saved an Empire"

ZAYN THE TENTH, ruler of the Omani Empire, enjoyed the finest of things. He ate the most expensive chocolates. His gardens—for he had several—were carefully tended and filled with the rarest of plants, and his reflecting pool contained only the most exotic fish from around the world. Sultan Zayn also enjoyed hosting parties—they were grand affairs, and royalty around the world waited eagerly each season to see if they would receive the trademark scroll embossed with the formal invitation. No one had ever declined. On the evenings of the parties, townspeople lined the roads for miles waving to passing carriages—everyone inside dressed in their finest suits, tunics, and gowns to match the theme of the season. One summer, the aesthetic had famously been floral, so men wore pink and pastel suits and the ladies wove roses and daisies into their hair. This winter, however, was a frosty theme, so everyone turned up in dazzling silvers and whites with diamonds dripping from fingers, necks, and ears.

And it was during that wintry evening ball, as the music flowed and the people danced, that a young man knocked on Sultan Zayn's palace door.

Prince Haris of Girad, a guest, looked on curiously as the butler opened the door, wondering which royal or dignitary might be arriving, but seeing a teenage boy with a face coated in grime, dirty matted hair, and clothes so flimsy from disrepair they looked as though they'd fall apart at the slightest touch, he wrinkled his nose in disgust.

"No beggars today, boy," the butler said firmly as he closed the door.

"Please, sir," the boy cried out. "I only need some water. A bit of bread. Whatever you could spare. I would work for it. I can scrub and clean. I can mend clothes. I'll do anything."

"Can't you see there's a party going on?" the butler said. "Come by tomorrow if you'd like, but the sultan will not be disturbed right now."

"Wait." Prince Haris walked over to where the boy stood on the marble front stoop. "You say you'll work for it, will you?"

"Yes, sir." The boy nodded.

"Then come on in." Prince Haris waved an arm. The boy hesitated, glancing at the butler before taking a tentative step inside.

"Up to your usual tricks, Haris?" A duchess walked over and winked.

"Boy says he wants to work for food." Haris shrugged. "Can't we at least segue this into some sort of entertainment? Can you juggle, boy?"

"No. . . ." The boy's gray eyes widened. "I didn't mean—"

"How about some death-defying tricks?" Haris moved closer to the boy. "Why don't you stand by the wall and see if we can throw some blades between your fingers and wager where they'll land? Or a dunking contest—take some bets on how long you can breathe underwater."

"I'd want in on that," a man said, approaching. Soon an audience had gathered.

The boy paled. He mumbled an apology. He took a step toward the door, but before he could leave, Haris shoved the boy.

"You said you'd work for money." Haris's eyes glimmered. "Said you'd do anything. You're a liar, then, aren't you? You know what I do to liars?"

But before the boy could say a word, Sultan Zayn strode through the crowd.

"What is going on here?" Zayn looked at the people around him, at Haris's expression, and then at the beggar's terrified face. "Is everything all right?"

"Just a little game." Haris shrugged. "This boy said he'd do anything for some food. Thought I'd make your ball a little more entertaining. Was doing you a favor, wasn't I, dear friend?"

"Do you find mocking a young man entertainment?" the sultan asked.

"Easy there," a woman laughed. "You know us, Zayn. We mean no harm. Were only having a bit of fun, weren't we?"

"But at whose expense?" The sultan frowned. "As my great-great-grandfather said, while the world is filled with kind and good people, the only way we can see a kind and good world is if we look beyond ourselves and intercede to help others when we can."

Zayn had a knapsack of food prepared for the boy—a bit of bread and chicken, a canteen of water, and dried fruits and nuts. Studying the boy's disheveled appearance, he asked, "Sleep on the ground, don't you?"

"Yes, Your Majesty," the boy said. "I have seven more days on my journey. Until then I sleep where and when I can, however I can."

"Get him something to lie upon at night, a blanket, a pillow," the sultan told the butler.

"For the beggar?" the butler sputtered. "We have only the finest things here, Your Majesty."

"Yes, for the *child*." Zayn nodded. "Get a pillow, blanket, and the rug from my old nursery. It's been gathering dust for decades anyhow—should be light enough to carry and sturdy enough for him to sleep on. And one of our maps, so he can navigate more easily."

The young boy stared at the bounty the sultan had given him.

"Thank you, Your Majesty." The boy's eyes brimmed with tears. "I will repay your kindness tenfold, this I promise you."

The sultan patted the boy on the shoulder and watched as he left the premises and disappeared into the night. It was a sweet gesture, the sultan thought as he rejoined the crowd, but the boy was young indeed if he thought he could ever be of help to a sultan such as himself.

• • — • •

Ten years hence, Zayn reflected back to the days of grand parties with a wistful twist in his heart. Gone were the days of embossed invitations and lavish affairs. His palace was in shambles—the roof on the southern wing of the estate shattered from the cannonade the enemy forces had rained upon them earlier in the week. That was when he'd told his men to lay down their weapons and sent a missive of their surrender to the other side, whose artillery they simply could not match. A handful of soldiers remained in the palace with him as they awaited the approaching army. They would be here soon. What a wonder, Zayn thought, how his kingdom had withstood centuries only to collapse under his watch. And as much as all this hurt, realizing how alone he truly was hurt far more.

There was a knock at the door.

So, this was it.

Once the door opened and he met the commander of the army face to face at last, he knew he would take his last breath.

A soldier moved to answer the door.

"No." Zayn stood up. "It should be me. The rest of you—you have served nobly and with honor. Do not try to defend me. Surrender and spare your families the pain of losing you."

But upon opening the door, Zayn did not see the gleaming smile of a military commander staring back at him; instead, it was a young man. His hair was dark and his eyes were gray.

"You," Zayn said slowly. "You're the boy from that day at the party."

"I am." The young man nodded. "I came to thank you for saving my life all those years ago. I was nearly done for; I had come to your doorstep out of complete desperation, never imagining anyone would truly help. Your kindness saved my life."

"I'm glad." Zayn glanced about at the dingy hall where once lanterns glowed and people danced. "Those days seem like a lifetime ago. My friends and allies abandoned me. A handful of tired soldiers and myself are all that are left of this kingdom."

"I am sorry to hear that," the man said.

"None are sorrier than I am. What has hurt the most in all of this, though, is realizing that the friendships and loyalties I had enjoyed and believed genuine were there only for my wealth and my power." The sultan sighed. "But that is neither here nor there. I'm glad time has done you well. But you aren't safe here—an army is fast approaching. It's better if you continue on your way."

"I saw the army." The man nodded. "They are a good five miles away but few in number. And I am here to assist you. I made a promise to help you someday, and that day has arrived. What if you found a way to outwit those who approach?" The man removed a map from his knapsack and presented it to the sultan.

Zayn frowned as he unfurled the map. It was the very

map he had given the boy all those years ago. He glanced down at his lands, at how vast they had been only ten years earlier.

"Thank you for this," Zayn said. "Though I'm afraid I have no use for it now."

"It's no longer an ordinary map," the man said. But before Zayn could ask him what he meant, the map began to glow, then shimmer, and then—

"The army." Zayn stared at the map. "I see them. Am I hallucinating?"

But he was not seeing things at all, for there on the scroll he could see the detachment of ten men on horseback making their way to the palace.

"I am of the magical realm," the man explained to the astonished sultan. "I had to flee my homeland because the people there did not handle our magic well, even if we only ever used it for good. They wanted to capture us and put us in a life of bondage as they do to genies. We've made a fine home for ourselves now, those of us who fled in time, and this map, woven now with my magic, is my gift to you. It will keep you abreast of the army's locations—any army present or future—and will light up hideaways for shelter and other ways to stay safe and secure during times of war. You may have lost many friends, Your Majesty, but you have my eternal loyalty—I am beholden to you not for the power or wealth you had but for your kindness. Please use this map—it will save your empire."

The soldiers gathered around the sultan and stared at the map, and then—they jumped up. They sheathed their swords against their waists and strapped their armor to their bodies. Their once-resigned expressions were now animated and full of life. The sultan looked down at the map; he did not know what was to come, but he knew now there was hope. And so, Zayn took his new magical map and strode out of the palace gates with his men to save their kingdom.

Jasmine

Chapter Five

*I*T TURNED OUT Ali had been right about the kingdom of Ababwa; it appeared to be *quite* the distance from the island. The carpet had slowed down a touch when they'd flown past the pyramids of Egypt and the Red Sea, but now they'd traveled so far that the darkness of night had lifted—here the sun was already halfway up in the sky.

"Are you sure this is okay?" she asked Ali. "I know visiting Ababwa was my idea, but hopefully we won't be too late getting back to Agrabah? If anyone noticed I was missing . . ."

"It hasn't been long at all," Ali reassured her. "The carpet flies fast. And time works differently when you've got a magic carpet by your side. Trust me, Princess." He smiled. "There's nothing to worry about. We can stay as long as you'd like."

Trust me. Jasmine studied him curiously. Those words again. It was simply a coincidence, she knew. Nothing more. And yet . . .

"You managing okay?" She looked down and petted the carpet. "Not too exhausted with flying around the world, are you?"

The carpet shook its tassels politely.

"The carpet has it covered," Ali said. "But we will make sure it gets plenty of rest once we reach the palace."

After seeming so hesitant to visit Ababwa when she'd first brought up the idea, he looked positively giddy about going home now.

A flash of gold glinted against the sun. Jasmine shielded her face with her hand and squinted. At first, she couldn't be sure what it was she was looking at, but as they flew closer she made out a golden minaret, then another—four of them in all. They were long and narrow with spiraling swirls etched along their spines, and so tall they jutted through the clouds.

"Is that your palace?" she asked, astonished. But what else could it be?

Pink birds with golden beaks and delicate silver patterns on their necks appeared nearby. The birds circled the carpet and somersaulted in the air before diving back to earth. She'd never seen anything like them before. Not even in books! But before she could ask Ali what sort of birds they were, the clouds parted and the kingdom of Ababwa came fully into view. One edge of the kingdom was bordered by a long stretch of craggy cliffs and coastline that looked undeveloped; it contained piles of rubble and towering boulders and was murky gray in color. Further inland, however, the kingdom proper looked to be set upon rolling green hills flanked by tall mountain peaks. Small lakes dotted the region. Peering down, she saw the palace at the center. Pathways wound up and sloped down past shops and cafés. A town square with an impressive fountain was not far from a pier lined with boats.

"That is some port." Jasmine gazed at the teal blue

water and the myriad of ships rolling over its surface. Agrabah had a fairly large dock for boats as well, but this one seemed to stretch out farther than she thought piers could possibly go. "And I'm not sure I've seen minarets quite that high up before," she told Ali as the carpet brought them slowly down. Now that they were lower, she saw rubies and emeralds encrusting the edges of the palace roof and windows. That was . . . interesting. "Your family spared no expense when they built this, huh?" she remarked.

But Ali didn't answer. And that's when she realized he hadn't responded to anything she'd said up to this point. Turning to look at him, she was surprised to see his lips slightly parted as he gazed at the sights below.

"Sorry." He flushed when he saw her looking at him. "Got distracted. But yeah, it is amazing, isn't it? I mean—" His flush deepened. "I should be more modest about it, I know, but . . ."

"It's been a while since you've been back?"

"You have no idea. I don't know how to describe it. It almost feels brand-new to me."

"That's kind of nice, isn't it? Helps you not take where you come from for granted."

"Couldn't have put it better myself, Princess."

As the carpet continued its descent, the cobblestoned roads came into clearer focus. The streets indeed climbed up and down the slopes and stretched out in all different directions from the leveled town center. Blue and red lanterns hung from metal poles that lined the roads at intervals. Beautiful awnings graced each storefront with the name of the shop and a corresponding illustration. An animal doctor, an apothecary, and other shops dotted the square.

No sooner did the carpet touch down just across the square than the seemingly idyllic town erupted with noise. People rushed out of their homes and stores, and soon a good-sized crowd surrounded them. Jasmine would have felt a bit intimidated by this were everyone not gazing at them with complete and utter adoration.

"Welcome back!" shouted a tall man. "It's been too long since you've been home, my prince."

A girl with curly hair approached Jasmine. She held a thick bouquet of pink and yellow flowers tied together with twine and handed them to Jasmine.

"Thank you." Jasmine took the bouquet from the child.

"These poppies grow all over the countryside. You can see them up and down the hills behind the town square," the girl said.

"They smell beautiful."

The girl clasped her hands in delight and hurried back to join the crowd.

"We're delighted to have you home," a woman called out. Some of the townspeople held out their hands toward the prince. Ali shook their hands and patted the young children on the head.

Jasmine wasn't sure if it was normal for people to be this ecstatic to see their prince return. She was fairly certain the people in Agrabah let out sighs of relief when her father traveled out of town with his constant companion, Jafar.

The thundering sound of hooves against gravel echoed in the distance. Jasmine looked up as they grew louder. Six majestic gray horses pulling a cream carriage embroidered with roses advanced. The crowd parted to make way for it to come through.

"That's for us?" Jasmine asked.

"I think so. I mean, yes," Ali said quickly.

The coachman wore a navy blue outfit with a matching

hat and expertly reined in the horses. They stopped just at Ali's feet. Hopping down, the coachman hurried over to open the carriage door for Jasmine and Ali.

"Welcome home, Prince Ali," he said. "We have missed you so."

The crowd erupted into applause so hearty the ground beneath them trembled. Ali blushed furiously.

The interior of the carriage was more spacious than it had appeared from the outside. The seats were velvet and the curtains were parted by silk ropes threaded with pearls. Jasmine trailed a finger across them, amazed to see they were genuine.

"Stay in my lap, Carpet," Ali told the magic rug as the horses began trotting and the carriage rumbled off. The carpet stuck its tassels out the window and twisted its body as though trying to squeeze out. "Of course you could fly us to the palace quickly," Ali reassured it, patting its side. "And I know it's not fun for you to be compressed into a small space like this. But please don't worry—you're safe here. Relax. You've earned it." The rug grudgingly complied and rested against Ali's lap. In just a few seconds, though Jasmine couldn't be sure, she'd have sworn the carpet was fast asleep.

Outside, people lined the cobblestoned walkways, waved, and shouted adulation at the passing carriage.

"They've really missed you," Jasmine observed, looking out the window at all the beaming faces.

"I guess it has been a while," Ali said. Jasmine studied him as he waved at his subjects. In her experience with the different royals who had come through Agrabah to try to win her hand, there were two types of princes. There was the one who looked bored and a bit irritated with all the attention from those he was in charge of ruling, leading, and providing for. And then there was the type of prince who preened and swelled practically to three times the size of a fully grown peacock when in the presence of mass adoration. But now she realized there was a third type, because Prince Ali was like neither of these types of men. He appeared taken aback and genuinely touched by the love of his subjects. It was more than just the fact that he hadn't been back to his kingdom in a while—he was truly humble. If she hadn't been here to witness it in person she wouldn't have believed such a thing was possible, but there it was. She hoped if she had the opportunity to become a ruler herself one day, she, too, could engender the respect and affection of her people as Prince Ali had.

"I think my arm is sore," Ali said. He leaned against the seat cushion now and stretched his arm before resting it against the carpet. He looked at Jasmine. "You look lost in your thoughts."

"I tend to always be lost in my thoughts," Jasmine replied. She looked around the carriage. "I guess I was thinking about how nice it is here. How admired you are in Ababwa. It's not like that for us back in Agrabah. Our subjects might throw a parade if we were to leave Agrabah, but certainly not when we returned."

"Maybe it has something to do with the guards?" Ali said. "They're stationed at practically every street corner . . . at least it looked like that when I was there. They walked among the people glaring at them a bit." He hesitated. "Sorry, I didn't mean to insult your kingdom, and I definitely don't want to stick my nose where it doesn't belong. It was just sort of the impression I got."

"Your impression was correct," she told him. "The guards really are everywhere. I've tried to talk to my father about it. It's not right to treat our citizens like they're guilty when they haven't done anything wrong. But Jafar—he's my father's advisor—he insists the guards need to be stationed throughout Agrabah to keep the peace. I wish he wouldn't have such a huge say, but my father trusts him completely. He doesn't understand that stationing guards on every street corner ends up sending a message that the leaders don't trust their people."

"No one wants to be made to feel guilty over nothing," Ali agreed. "What does your father have to say about it when you discuss it with him?"

"I never get the chance to talk to him about it alone."

"Jafar is always there?"

"Yes. If I could talk to my father by myself, things could be different. He's seemed open-minded when I've brought up changes we should make in the past, but as soon as Jafar shows up, the conversation ends."

"But you're his daughter. You have every right to speak alone in confidence with your father whenever you want to."

Ali was right about that. If she ever became sultana, she'd start with a bit of housecleaning and get a new advisor, first and foremost. Even if Agrabah would never have citizens who adored their rulers the way the ones here in Ababwa appeared to adore Ali, they had to do better than they were.

When Jasmine looked out the window again, she paused.

Goosebumps trailed her shoulders. They tickled the back of her neck. It was easy to miss the man amid the crowd of happy villagers chatting and talking over one another as they waved at the passing carriage. One's eyes could simply pass right over him, mistaking him for a statue on the street corner. But he was no statue. He was a man. His clothing was tattered and torn. His face was coated in grime. But it was none of this that made Jasmine's stomach clench. It was the fact that among a sea of admiring gazes, this man alone scowled at them. His gray eyes were narrowed; a deep frown line creased his forehead. He didn't simply look at the passing carriage. He glared at it. Their eyes met then. He cocked his head to the side and stared at her. Looking into his eyes turned her insides cold.

It was the strangest thing. The man seemed familiar. But where could she have seen him before? It was impossible. Wasn't it?

The carriage jerked to a stop.

"Whoa!" Ali's head bumped against the window.

"Did we hit something?" Jasmine asked, holding onto the window.

"My apologies," the coachman called out. He opened the carriage door. "The horses were not eager to stop their ride. We are at the palace now."

The carriage door opened wider and Ali stepped down. He reached back and held his hand up to Jasmine. "Ready, Princess?"

Jasmine glanced back out the window, but there was simply empty space now where the man had once stood. He was gone.

"Saw something interesting?" Ali asked her.

"No . . . it was nothing."

Taking his hand, she stepped onto the road. Together they approached the palace gates and the golden estate just beyond the brick walls.

Aladdin

Chapter Six

PLAY IT COOL, Aladdin reminded himself. After all, theoretically, he'd seen all these sights before. This was his home. If one lived on the moon, even that would get dull after a lifetime. He had to act like all of this was commonplace and ordinary.

But how?

Ababwa seemed plucked straight out of his deepest dreams. The town square they'd passed on the ride over had a public fountain for the village's poor. He hadn't even told Genie about that and yet there it was—a gathering place where people replenished their buckets right before his eyes. And then there were the thick leafy palm trees flanking each side of the road they had traveled down—he loved those trees! And the way the entire town seemed to have a hint of warmth emanating from it. Everything about Ababwa felt tailor-made for him. Which, he realized with a start, it was.

He was trying his best to act natural, but glancing at Jasmine, he wasn't sure how well that was working out. And as they approached the palace—ostensibly his house—he knew acting natural here would be his biggest challenge yet.

Two guards stood on either side of the steel gates outside the palace walls. Their muscled arms were crossed as they stood at attention. They were so tall they towered over him. Aladdin tensed and instinctively reached for Jasmine's hand. They looked much like the men who patrolled the streets of Agrabah with their sharp jaws and stoic expressions. Even though Aladdin knew they were *his* guards and that they were not standing there to grab him or throw him into prison, he glanced about for possible escape routes. But their expressions melted into smiles upon seeing Aladdin, and they nodded before opening the wrought iron gate for him and Jasmine. Aladdin felt a palpable sense of relief. As they headed up the steps, two servants parted the front doors before they could even knock.

"This is . . ." Jasmine looked around as they stepped into the foyer. "This is quite the entrance."

"Thanks," Aladdin said. She was right. The molding around the ceiling was filled with glittering jewels, as were the baseboards. A fountain was on display in the center of the entryway. Water splashed from the mouth of a carved ceramic dolphin. *Well done, Genie,* Aladdin thought.

He took in the red silk carpets running from one end of the room to the other. The crystal chandeliers. Marble floors. None of this was really his, Aladdin knew. They were here only for a brief visit. But as long as they *were* here, everything from the gold-encrusted minarets to the fountain at his feet belonged to him. After a lifetime of struggling to scrape by, to simply make sure he and Abu had enough to eat that day, it was the strangest feeling to stand before unimaginable wealth and claim it as his own. Aladdin smiled; as long as he was here, he might as well enjoy it.

They headed into a hall where an oversized floor-to-ceiling oil portrait of Aladdin dressed in full princely regalia atop a snowy horse hung on the wall. Aladdin's arms were crossed and his chin was at a tilt as he looked down regally upon them. Now *that* was an impressive painting. He grinned.

"Oh!" Jasmine nearly jumped back when she saw it. She paused. "It's quite a large painting, isn't it?"

"It really is! Thanks!"

"Welcome back, Prince Ali," said a man approaching them now. He had a white mustache and graying hair and wore a navy kaftan with a matching round hat atop his head. Aladdin faltered a bit upon seeing him. His uncle—his mother's older brother—had died when Aladdin was quite young, but the mustache and hair reminded him so much of the stories his mother had shared of him. Walking up to Aladdin now, the man opened his arms wide and embraced him. It was strangely comforting. As if they'd known each other a lifetime.

The man smiled at Jasmine and folded his hands in greeting. "Princess Jasmine. A pleasure to meet you. My name is Omar. I am Prince Ali's butler."

"Wonderful to meet you," Jasmine said. "Have you been at this palace long?"

"I've been working here most of my life," Omar said. "I looked out for Prince Ali when he was a child. Now that he is all grown up, I assist however I can."

"Interesting." She glanced at Aladdin and then back at Omar. "If you've known Ali his whole life, then you would be the keeper of his stories? All the embarrassing ones he'd prefer left unsaid?" Her eyes sparkled mischievously.

"I have a treasure trove of stories—just say the word." Omar winked. "I am quick to spill my secrets."

"Hey, now," Aladdin protested while they laughed. He wondered what sort of stories a fictional person in an imaginary land would have to share about him.

"Please allow me to escort you to the dining room," the man said now. "Everyone is waiting for you."

Everyone?

They walked down the main hall until they reached a spacious room showcasing not one, two, or even three, but *four* staircases inlaid with silver winding several stories above them. Outside the oversized windows flanking the far wall, lush green grounds stretched out into the distance with trimmed shrubbery in animal shapes lining the walkways.

Just then, servants in matching navy uniforms entered the room in single file and stood with their backs against the wall at full attention.

"Princess Jasmine, it would be my honor to introduce you to our palace staff," Omar said. One by one he told Jasmine—as well as Aladdin himself—each person's name and role in keeping the palace up and running. The stout man with the tall white hat was the chef. The woman next to him with wavy hair and a measuring tape draped around her neck was the palace tailor. Next came the gardeners—ten of them in all—and the housecleaning staff, the palace barber, and so on. Omar introduced them all.

"We have the most wonderful meal prepared for both of you," the chef told them.

"Oh, you shouldn't have gone through all that trouble," Aladdin said.

"Not at all! It was exciting to have a grand feast to prepare! As soon as we heard you'd arrived, everyone got to work at once. You will not be disappointed." The chef clasped his hands together and hurried into the kitchen.

As it turned out, the chef was right.

The polished oak table in the dining room had a scarlet runner that stretched from one end of the table to the other. Jasmine and Aladdin sat next to one another and watched servants set out plate after plate of food while the chef told them about each dish—piping hot breads, gourmet cheeses, and jams handmade from fruit grown on the palace grounds. The pastries featured olives and greens plucked from the grounds of the palace as well.

"What else could they possibly be bringing?" Jasmine laughed when the kitchen doors swung open once more. A woman walked out balancing a wooden tray with six different steaming porcelain teapots and matching teacups. Aladdin started when he saw that they were decorated with tulips. His mother had once found tulip teacups among the discards someone had placed outside their home. She'd cleaned them up nicely, and they'd used them for years. Of course, the cups they'd had weren't quite so fancy; he smiled wanly, remembering the chipped edges and faded designs. His heart filled with gratitude for this personal touch Genie had added.

"The tea smells divine," Jasmine said.

"Thank you." The woman smiled. "I have ginger, mint,

oolong, peppermint, rose petal, and orange berry. But we have more, so please don't hesitate to ask."

"The ones you have brought all sound marvelous," Jasmine said. She looked at Aladdin. "Which would you like?"

"Um . . ." Aladdin hesitated, then picked up the one in front of him. "This one?"

"Good choice," Jasmine said. "You can never go wrong with mint."

He poured some in his cup and took a sip.

"Not bad," Aladdin said, unable to hide his surprise.

"I see the princess inspired Prince Ali to try some tea," Omar noted from where he stood by the far wall.

"Inspired?" Jasmine glanced at Aladdin. "Does he not normally enjoy tea?"

"Not after what happened many a moon ago."

"Really?" Jasmine lowered her teacup. "Now I have to know the story."

"Um," Aladdin interrupted, "she doesn't need to hear that."

"Now I *really* need to." Jasmine laughed. "Please, Omar, go on."

"Sorry, Prince Ali. But I cannot refuse the request

of a princess," Omar said, his eyes twinkling. "His dislike for tea began young, but it's not the tea that was to blame. He was a little boy of five back then. Some royal guests arrived to visit the family and Prince Ali insisted on helping. He was getting into just about everything, so his mother ushered him over to the kitchen to help the staff with the tea—stirring sugar. Simple enough. Our young boy was eager to get to work, though there was a slight hiccup since he could not yet read labels, and . . . well, in fairness, salt and sugar *are* the same color. . . ."

"Oh, no," Jasmine clasped a hand to her mouth to stifle a laugh.

"Oh, yes." Omar nodded gravely. "Our young prince stirred salt into all the tea, including his own. And when the time came to serve their guests, well, everyone had a most unexpected surprise."

"Poor Ali," Jasmine said. "That might have put me off tea for good as well."

"Yeah." Aladdin managed to smile. He shifted in his seat. It wasn't that Omar had shared an embarrassing childhood tale with Jasmine that unsettled him . . . it was the fact that the story Omar shared was true. Of course, the people who had been visiting his mother and him that day were friends passing through town, not royalty. And there were no servants; Aladdin was helping his mother herself prepare the tea. He could still remember the laughing and conversations as everyone had sat in his family's humble dwelling, and then the sudden shock in their eyes when they'd tasted their drinks. He hadn't reflected upon that memory in years.

Suddenly, a banging sound jolted Aladdin from his memory.

"What was that?" Jasmine jumped at the noise.

"Let me in! Right now!" a loud angry voice shouted in the distance.

"That doesn't sound good," Jasmine murmured as the banging continued.

"I'll see what the matter is." Aladdin stood up.

"No, Your Majesty, please relax." Omar sighed. "It's a man—he came by earlier, just before you arrived. An eager subject wanting to welcome his prince home, I suppose. But he'll meet you in due time. Please enjoy your meal. I'll go speak to him again. If you'll excuse me." With that, Omar turned and walked out of the room.

Aladdin wondered if he should follow; what would a

real prince do in such a situation? But he decided Omar would come get him if he were needed.

Birds chirped outside the window across from them. He watched as a chickadee fluttered up and disappeared into a birdhouse perched on a wooden pole just beyond a patch of shrubbery.

"Hope you didn't mind Omar sharing that story," Jasmine said.

"No, no." Aladdin turned to look back at her, shaking his head. "It had been a long time since I had heard it, actually."

"Where *are* your parents?" Jasmine asked. "Are they traveling these days?"

Aladdin put his teacup down and swallowed. "They died."

"Both of them?" Jasmine put her own tea down and turned toward him.

"I was young when it happened. First my father. A few years later, my mother."

"Oh, Ali. I lost my mother years ago; I can't imagine how painful it must be to lose both of your parents."

"It was a long time ago. I don't remember much."

"Doesn't mean you miss them any less, I'm sure."

She was right about that.

"So, all of this"—she gestured to the room—"the palace and the grounds. This entire kingdom. It's all yours?"

"Yes. I don't have any family left in the world."

Jasmine's eyes brimmed with tears. Aladdin cleared his throat.

"I'm never wanting for company, though," he said quickly. This was true; after all, Abu was like family. And now he had the carpet, and Genie. "And I have so many responsibilities—I'm too busy to think much about it."

"Does that make you the king of Ababwa, if you are the sole heir?"

"Oh, right. Well. I'm the ruler, so I'm *effectively* the king," he said, improvising. "But I can't be officially king until my twenty-fifth birthday. So until then I'm a prince." He flinched as the words left his mouth. He knew it was unavoidable, but he hated lying to her.

"When you lose your parent, there's a part of you that remains missing," Jasmine said. "It doesn't go away. You just learn how to live with it."

Aladdin nodded. He knew just what she meant. "I was only a few years old when my father died. I have almost no memories of him except some fuzzy recollections. But I was about seven years old when my mother died from a lengthy illness. I remember her more than my father, but with each passing day, when I close my eyes and think of her, the memories fade a bit more. I hate that. I have some memories, but they're not enough." He blinked. He'd never said so much about all of this to anyone. Jasmine was so easy to talk to. The way she listened—it was a new feeling. He liked it.

"Memories have a way of losing their edges as time passes."

"What was she like, your mother?" Aladdin asked.

"She was lovely," Jasmine said. "She was from Shirabad, which she ruled long before she met my father. She traveled back and forth all the time. Sometimes I went with her."

"So she let you travel."

"Oh, yes. She wasn't anything like my father. He's so afraid to lose me, he won't let me live. I was supposed to become a ruler like her. I'd linger in her quarters for hours listening as she met with her advisors and brokered peace agreements between nations. She let me observe and absorb it all because I was meant to follow in her footsteps. I never met anyone who was as natural a leader as she was. If she knew the way I was living now, she would be livid."

"She sounds amazing," Aladdin said.

"She was. But I guess it's not her leadership I miss most. It's all the rest of it. The things that wouldn't matter to anyone else except for me. Like how she tucked me in at night with my favorite lullaby. The way she held my hand until I was asleep. The sound of her laughter. But even then . . ." Her eyes grew misty. "Even with all of these memories, I want more. Memories can't replace the person you miss."

Aladdin thought of his mother. Even when she was alive they'd still been poor. But despite all they didn't have, having one another had always felt like enough. Even now, he could remember his mother's deep brown eyes, so dark they looked black if you didn't pay close enough attention.

He gazed around the room, and then his eyes landed on a pair of golden-framed portraits at the far end. They hung adjacent to where Jasmine and Aladdin sat in the dining room. He straightened, blinking. It couldn't be. His eyes were playing tricks on him. But there they were, against the gold-papered walls: two floor-to-ceiling oil portraits. And the people in those portraits looked like his mother and father.

He walked toward the portraits as though in a trance. Jasmine followed close behind. She didn't say a word. Face to face now, there was no doubt about who those people in the frames were. His mother wore a taffeta and lace sage-green blouse. Her hair was wrapped in a bun and she wore a diamond tiara. His father held a staff in his hand and peered down at them with sparkling green eyes—it was almost as though he were truly looking at them. Aladdin remembered his father's eyes. When so much had faded from his memories of the man, he'd remembered that much. Now he saw that his father had the same brown skin and square jawline as Aladdin's own.

He knew his parents had probably never worn clothing like this, but beneath the royal garb, he felt the warmth of their smiles, which seemed truer than anything in the world.

"You have her eyes," Jasmine said. "And his smile."

Aladdin nodded, unable to speak.

"You okay?" Jasmine asked gently.

"It's just that I haven't seen their faces in some time."

He turned to Jasmine. "Do you ever wonder what your life would have been like if your mother had still been a part of it?"

"All the time."

Until Aladdin had met Jasmine, he'd assumed people who lived in palaces, with every material thing they could ever desire at their fingertips, did not want for anything. But all the gold and riches in the world could not bring back Jasmine's mother or his own parents. Jasmine had so many memories of her mother. Far more memories than he had of his own parents. Did it hurt less to have fewer memories? Did the loss not sting as deep? Or did it not make a difference at all, because whether the memories of those you'd lost were many or few, it didn't change how much you loved them?

"Wish I could have met them," Jasmine said.

"Me too," said Aladdin. Jasmine looked up at him, and then, she reached out, took his hand in hers, and squeezed it gently. Just like that, Aladdin's heart felt a bit less heavy. He knew their actual stations in life were worlds apart, but even with the different lives they had led, she understood him like no one else ever had. The past could not be undone. But when he looked down at her hand in his, and then into her beautiful wide brown eyes—for the first time in a long while, he thought seriously about the future. It was still unwritten. Normally all the uncertainty of that would fill him with anxiety, but right now, hand in hand with Princess Jasmine, the endless possibilities ahead felt like a wonderful thing indeed.

Jasmine

Chapter Seven

JASMINE AND ALI stepped through the wide glass doors that overlooked the grand sitting room and into the main courtyard of the palace. In contrast to the rest of the opulent palace, this courtyard was a breath of fresh air—simple and elegant. The walls were graced with murals of flowers and butterflies and birds designed intricately out of geometric shapes; flowers in pastel pots dotted the perimeter and trailed onto a wide-open pathway that looked like it led into the sprawling gardens and grounds of the palace.

"Now, this is nice," she said. "This might be my favorite spot in your home! From what I've seen so far, that is."

"I'm glad you like it." Ali ran his hands along a wall of tiles layered into the image of a soaring white sparrow. "This is my favorite also. I designed it myself not too long ago."

Jasmine felt bad that she hadn't found much to compliment about the rest of his home. But the truth was that it was all so *incredibly* over the top. She was all for a nice flight of stairs, but was there really a place in any palace for *four* jewel-encrusted staircases? And those enormous minarets surrounding the building—why would someone go through all the trouble and put people at risk getting those things so high up like that? Surely it was also a hazard for the birds that flew about the kingdom. And then there was that ridiculous portrait of Ali grinning down upon any passerby from the foyer as though he just might leap out of the frame and wrestle them. Why would anyone commission a painting like that of themselves, much less hang it up as the first image guests saw when they entered the palace? She looked at the man next to her now; she couldn't imagine him ever posing as pompously as that.

She knew her mother would have chided her for her uncharitable thoughts. "Be careful not to judge others simply because their worldview is different from your own," she had often reminded Jasmine. "Others have not lived your life, just as you have not lived theirs."

Jasmine knew her mother was right about this. For starters, Jasmine had never lived a life where a magic carpet could whisk her from island to city to country to continent in a matter of seconds. Even now she could scarcely believe all the things she'd seen. And the truth was that as over-the-top as this palace might have been, Ali himself was anything but. He was down to earth and kind and warm. He spoke to everyone he met, regardless of their occupation or social standing, without a trace of affectation or pretense. It was no wonder they'd lined the streets to greet him with so much adoration when the two of them had arrived. She couldn't hold it against him that his ancestors had taste that didn't exactly align with contemporary palace standards, could she? She knew what it was like to have to live with the choices others had made. And as for the smug, smiling portrait—well, no one was perfect.

"Do we have time for a stroll through the palace

grounds?" she asked him. "They extend quite far into the distance, it looks like."

"Absolutely," Ali told her. "And there's something I want to show you out there that I just know you're going to love."

"Oh? What is it?"

"Can't tell you. It's a surprise!"

"No, no," she protested. "There's something you should know about me. I really don't like surprises."

"All right, fair enough." He laughed. "Why don't we go ahead and head over there right now, in that case?"

Just then, a door flew open and slammed behind them. Heavy footsteps approached. Ali gripped Jasmine's hand and swiveled to see who it was. Upon finding that it was Omar hurrying over to them, he relaxed, his grip loosening.

She studied him curiously. Who had Ali thought was approaching them? And why did he appear so tense? She'd noticed the same look pass across his face when they'd walked up to the palace guards earlier—he had grabbed her hand then, too, and looked as though he were preparing to bolt at any second.

"Pardon me, Your Highness," Omar apologized to

Jasmine before turning to Ali. "Prince Ali, I have come to remind you about your meeting today. It starts in just about five minutes."

"What meeting?" Ali asked him.

"The constituency council meeting you have every month with your people, my prince. Everyone is so excited you are back in time for this month's open forum. People do rely on your advice so very much, and they've missed it lately what with your being away so much with all your travels."

"Oh, right," Ali said. "The constituency council. I had forgotten all about that."

"You have an open forum with your subjects every month?" Jasmine asked. "Anyone can come and talk to you there?"

"I love helping people out and knowing what the issues may be in Ababwa." Ali nodded. "I think it's important for people who are charged with ruling a kingdom to listen to their subjects and give whatever advice to their troubles that they can offer, but . . ." He turned to Omar. "The thing is that I'm only here for a quick trip to show Jasmine the kingdom. I can reschedule the meeting for when I return next time. Would that be all right?"

"Of course, I will send them away and postpone it. Whatever you would like." Omar hesitated. "But my prince, allow me to be so bold as to ask you to reconsider. They've been lining up outside the meeting room since they heard of your return. They are so eager to see you."

"Well . . ." Ali sighed.

"It's entirely your decision, Prince Ali. I can send them away if you would like. I am sure they will understand."

"Don't hold off on having this meeting on my account," Jasmine said at once.

"Are you sure?" Ali asked her.

"Work comes first, and this is such important work. To listen to your subjects in this way—it must make such a difference."

Ali studied her for a moment. "Want to join me?"

"I'd love to." She nodded. "Gives me a chance to learn how this whole thing works."

"Not to learn." Ali shook his head. "I mean, would you be willing to sit alongside me and help advise? Two heads are better than one, right?"

"You want my help with advising your people?" Jasmine asked.

"Only if you want to," Prince Ali quickly hurried to

add. "If you'd rather rest or take in the gardens while I finish that meeting, I understand."

"No, it's not that. It's just that no one has ever asked me to be part of any serious decision-making before. I . . . I would be honored, of course," she finally said. "Thank you."

"Thank *you* for being so understanding about this and for offering to share your insights." He turned to Omar. "Can we get her an extra seat next to mine?"

"Of course," Omar said. "I will arrange for it at once. And, oh!" He paused, reaching into a satchel by his side. "I almost forgot—your bag."

Ali frowned at the gray pouch lined with gold thread that Omar proffered now. Ali looked at it but did not move to take it.

"Your satchel, sir," Omar said, his hand still outstretched. "I forgot to give it to you when you first arrived. But I know you like to have it with you in case it becomes necessary."

Ali took the bag from him and opened it. Jasmine saw a glint of gold from within and heard the sound of metal clinking.

"Thanks for remembering." Ali looked relieved. "I'm

all mixed up today, aren't I?" He quickly tied the pouch to a loop on his waist. He turned to Jasmine now. "Shall we head over to advise the people?" Ali offered his arm to her.

"Let's." Jasmine took his arm. "So," she said as they walked toward the palace, "tell me a little about this surprise."

"Can't do that. It won't be a surprise then."

"Oh, come on, at least a hint?"

"Nope. Sorry. It will spoil the fun."

"Fun? The suspense is unbearable!" she protested.

"Well, now I *have* to keep it under wraps." Ali laughed. "The suspense will make the discovery all the more exciting."

"Fine." Jasmine rolled her eyes. "I can wait."

Arm in arm, they headed back to the palace. They were both so taken by the courtyard's murals and potted plants, and with one another, that neither of them noticed him—the man peering through the wrought iron gates just on the other side of the courtyard. And neither of them saw this stranger carefully watch them returning to the palace, his eyes narrow. His expression darkening.

Aladdin

Chapter Eight

*T*HE ADVISORY HALL—that's what Omar had called it when they walked in—was not so much a hall as practically a palace in its own right. A freestanding white brick building, it sat just off to the side of the courtyard. Inside, the walls were a cool gray, and paintings of the kingdom of Ababwa with its sloping green hills and images of the town square they'd passed by earlier were encased in silver and gold frames, hanging at even intervals all around them. Aladdin took in the cliffside gardens and butterflies in one painting and the lagoon in the other. Genie had indeed created a most enchanting place.

The two of them sat atop a raised stage on matching plush chairs with tall gold backings. The magic carpet lay at their feet, resting and still. To their right was a wooden podium and a carpet runner that snaked all the way to the oak doors at the far end of the room. Aladdin could hear conversations from outside, and though he could not make out what they were saying, he could tell from the frenetic energy that Omar was right—the people on the other side of that door were eager to meet with him.

He understood why Genie had come up with this meeting idea. Aladdin *had* told him he wanted to be a source of advice and comfort to the people in his kingdom. And while Aladdin appreciated this attention to detail, glancing over at Jasmine now, he hoped she couldn't tell just how anxious he felt. It was one thing to want to help people with their problems but another thing to actually *do* it. What if he couldn't? He had no experience in such things. It didn't matter that they weren't real people, because Jasmine believed them to be so. Whatever advice he gave for their imagined challenges and troubles would reflect upon whether he possessed leadership qualities. His words would matter to Jasmine. He had to get it right.

"Are you ready, Prince Ali?" Omar asked. He stood by the front door and held on to its brass handle.

Aladdin nodded. There was no use in putting off the inevitable. He risked a quick glance at Jasmine, hoping she couldn't sense his nerves. But she was looking ahead eagerly.

Aladdin turned back to see Omar had opened the door. The line began right at the front of the door and stretched out of his field of vision.

"How many people are there?" Aladdin managed to ask.

"Not many," Omar assured him. "I'd say about fifty. Not more than that."

"Oh," Aladdin said weakly. "That's all?"

A woman approached the podium first and looked down at the ground as she spoke. A brown shawl was draped around her shoulders. "Prince Ali, I come here today with grave worry in my heart. My father is ill."

"I'm sorry to hear that," Aladdin said. "What is his ailment?"

"Headaches," she said. "They're so bad he can't work

or eat properly. The local apothecary in the town square has managed to find a concoction that works quite well, but the herbs are precious and two gold coins each week is more than we can afford."

The woman looked so familiar, Aladdin thought. The rings of exhaustion that circled her eyes made her look much like a tired neighbor he'd known when he was younger. She, too, had cared for a family member who suffered from migraines. She'd spent her days working and her nights tending to her sick father.

"I was wondering if there's work you may need done at the palace," the woman continued. "I am a good seamstress and I clean very well. Cook, too. I'd be ever so grateful for the opportunity."

Aladdin admired the woman's sense of pride. His own mother had been the same way.

"I appreciate your offer of help, but we have everything covered here," Aladdin told her, thinking of the line of servants he'd met upon their arrival. "However . . ." He reached into the satchel attached to his belt, buried within the folds of his clothing, and pulled out some coins that he offered to Omar. He was careful not to disturb the lamp, which had also been tucked into the satchel. He presumed Genie had sent it along in case of emergencies, but it made him a little nervous to have it here in Ababwa. He didn't want to disturb it or let Jasmine or anyone else see it.

Omar took the coins from Aladdin and handed them to the woman. She stared at the money.

"I don't understand," she said slowly.

"Is it enough?" Aladdin asked. "I can give you more if you need to tide yourself over for a little while longer."

"Y-y-yes, it is enough. N-n-no, I don't need more. But sir, I can't." She shook her head. "I am capable of working for it. I want to."

"I appreciate your work ethic," Aladdin told her. "But sometimes we need help, and we have to be strong enough to accept it. Especially when it's a matter of grave importance. You need to care for your family. When things are better, you can help others, and in this way, the work continues. Would those be acceptable terms?"

"I will never . . ." The woman's voice choked up. "I will never be able to repay you for your generosity. Yes. Once I can get back on my feet—I will pass this generosity you have offered me onward. In whatever way that I can, I will. I swear it, Prince Ali. Thank you." The woman clasped her hands to her chest in gratitude before leaving.

"That was very generous," Jasmine told him once the woman had left.

"I know money won't solve all the problems that come through this door, but sometimes all people need is a break when they need it most."

"Giving money to people when they need it is a very kind gesture." She hesitated. "But is there a system in place for people like this that could help further?"

"A system?"

"I've read about something similar in one of my favorite books. It's about legendary leaders," she said. "I read in there that some kingdoms have free clinics. They pay for doctors and herbalists to set aside time every week to meet the needs of those who cannot afford such things on their own. Once that woman runs out of that money, she may still need more assistance—and it was so difficult for her to accept what you gave her as it was, who knows if she'd come to ask again? A free clinic could be a way to not only help her get the regular assistance she'll most likely need, but it could help others throughout the kingdom. It's something I've been trying to talk to my father about for our own kingdom, in fact."

"That's a great idea," Aladdin said, touched to know Jasmine was trying to do this for Agrabah. He could only imagine what a service like that could have done for his mother when she had fallen ill with no means to pay for medicine or a doctor's visit.

The next people who approached the podium had simple enough issues. Two neighbors bickering about a shared water pump they'd installed between their homes; each neighbor believed the other used it more. Aladdin smiled a bit. This very issue was one his friends back in Agrabah had once had. Just as he had back home, Aladdin drew up an equitable schedule for them to put up in their homes. Of course, back in Agrabah, the schedule was written on a scrap of paper and not on a fancy papyrus scroll, but the end result was still the same: both men walked away pleased.

The next two people who arrived were disagreeing about a fence one of them was planning to install.

"He's trying to build up a wall," the woman complained. "Yes, it's his property, I'm not arguing the legality of it—but it is the fastest path for me to get to the town square. To do this now, at my old age? It's downright cruel, my prince."

"Wouldn't need to put up a fence if your goats didn't chew up my gardens," the man snapped. "I should be charging *you* to put up the fence!"

"There are no other ways to stop the goats besides putting up a fence?" Aladdin asked.

"I tried roping them in," the woman said. "But they chewed right through the ropes. Had a metal enclosure for them, but they managed to break that down as well."

"That's why I got the sturdy kind of fence coming up now," the man said, nodding.

"But they're just sweet little babes. If they eat a vegetable now and then, what's the harm? How many cheeses have I given you over the years out of neighborly affection? That fence is going to add an extra twenty minutes to my trips into town. You know how my knees ache."

Aladdin turned to Jasmine. "Any ideas?" he asked her.

"Me?" Jasmine looked startled for a second. "Is it okay for me to intrude?"

"Intrude? I welcome your wisdom, Princess."

Jasmine thought for a moment and then turned to the people.

"I understand the predicament," she said. "Nothing is stopping those goats, and a fence may be the only way. Your neighbor is entitled to not have his hard work eaten."

"See?" The man glared at the woman.

"But it's also unfortunate this means she'll have to walk so far to get to town," Jasmine continued. "It was so nice of you to allow her to pass through your property all these years."

"I wish I didn't have to do this." The man's expression softened. "But the goats can't be stopped any other way."

"Perhaps a gate?" Jasmine asked. "Once the fence is up, a gate could help her come to and from while keeping your land secure."

"I had thought about that," the man said. "But that would cost far more money than I can manage. Putting the fence up is difficult enough."

"Perhaps you can pay for the cost of the gate?" Aladdin suggested to the woman. "May be worth it."

"I suppose that's fair," the woman said grudgingly.

"I'll ask the workers about adding one once I get back," the man said. Both walked away satisfied.

"You doing all right?" Aladdin asked Jasmine after the

thirty-eighth query. The line was moving steadily, but it had been a while. "You can always take a break or go rest in one of the guest suites while I finish up."

"And miss all of this?" Jasmine exclaimed. "I'm going to tell my father all about how well it's all working here in Ababwa when I get back. We need to have meetings like this with our own subjects back home."

"But you've never been to Ababwa, right?" Aladdin winked.

"Oh. That's right . . ." Jasmine said. Her smile faded a bit.

"I was only teasing," Aladdin said quickly.

"No, it's just that you *are* right. I can't tell him about any of this. It's awful how much I can't share with him." She sighed. "But I can still tell him about this idea. Even if I can't tell him how I know it would work so well."

Aladdin flushed at the praise. It felt good to know that because of the time they'd spent together, Jasmine might be able to encourage her father to implement something similar in Agrabah. This trip could possibly lead to real change back home. Agrabah would benefit from its subjects being heard. That much was certain.

A woman approached the podium next. A small boy

was draped across her like a blanket, his arms limp at his sides, his head burrowed in the crook of her neck. Aladdin understood before she spoke why this woman had come.

"My name is Maha." The woman trembled. "This is my son, Usman. I'm not even sure why I'm here for a matter that advice cannot possibly fix, but"—her eyes welled with tears—"if there was even a small chance something could be done to help my child, I had to try."

"I understand it's hard to ask for help," Aladdin said gently. "Please tell us. What is the nature of your son's illness?"

"Fevers. He gets high fevers that leave him unable to do anything at all. Even sips of water require effort."

"Do you need money for a doctor?" Aladdin reached for his coin purse. He thought of Jasmine's idea for a clinic.

"We've taken him to many different doctors. Nothing can be done. He had these fevers as a baby, but they went away. Now, with the weather so warm of late, the illness returned. We put cool washcloths on him, keep him in the shade—nothing helps. And when he's feverish he won't eat, and when he won't eat he can't function, and then . . . well, what will become of my boy?" She let out a sob. "My husband and I are awning makers. It's our livelihood, but we can't work while he's so sick. People say they understand the delays, but they will lose their patience soon enough. And less money from the work being done means less resources for us to feed our family. It's . . . difficult."

"I understand," Aladdin said. He knew all too well how quickly an illness could leave a family destitute. But what on earth could he say to this woman to help her?

"I'm sorry about your son," Jasmine said. "Have you spoken with the local apothecary? Someone had come earlier and mentioned that they are a bit pricey, but good at finding cures."

"They tried many different concoctions, but none of them work. The local herbalist tried as well." She paused. "I'm sorry for wasting your time. No one can help me. I suppose I just felt desperate." She turned to leave.

"Wait," Aladdin called out. "Maha, don't leave yet. Just give me a moment. I want to help you."

But how?

Maha stood to the side as another woman marched up to the podium. Her hair flowed dark against her shoulders, on her arm dangled a gilded cage filled with the most unusual bees. They were the size of a clenched fist, their gold-and-black bodies shimmering as though they had been dipped in glitter when they fluttered back and forth.

"They're moving very slowly," Jasmine observed.

"Yes, Princess, they are," the woman responded. Indeed, it was true. While they were lovely to behold, Aladdin didn't need to ask why the woman was here. Even from where he was sitting he could see the bees were not well. They spun about in circles as though dizzy, crashing into one another. "My name is Zaria, and I came here because my bees are dying. They need your help."

"What happened to them?"

"The heat," the woman explained. "I once had colonies of thousands of bees. They are usually quite strong; they can even sting without dying. But now I'm down to a handful. These bees are the healthy ones I could bring along to show you."

"They are honey bees?" Jasmine asked.

"Yes." She nodded. "They are also my life's work. These bees make medicinal honey that can heal people. It cures ailments no other medicine can, and now it's all coming to an end because each season is hotter than the last. They drop like flies; they're not made for the heat like this. They managed to at least hold on in the past, but lately their natural habitat, the olive trees behind our home, are losing their leaves. The canopy had kept them shaded, but the leaves have been blistering and falling off because of the weather."

"The bees can't be moved indoors?"

"I tried that when I got desperate enough, but it didn't work. They need the outdoors and sunlight like they need air. It's just their temperament. We've been fanning them around the clock, but it doesn't make a lick of difference."

"Has the local veterinarian had a chance to see them?"

"She's tried her best," Zaria said. "But as I mentioned, these are one-of-a-kind bees, and the last of their kind at that. There isn't much anyone can really do to cure them. Don't know why I came, really." She shifted the cage to her other arm. "Suppose I wanted someone to just hear my pain, is all."

"I know how that is," Maha said. Her son was still asleep on her shoulder. "Talking about what ails won't necessarily fix things, but there is solace in being heard."

Aladdin swallowed. Two people in a row whom he could not help. He knew not all problems had solutions, but it was a heavy realization when he was the one who was supposed to be doing the solving.

"The bees make honey that heal people, right?" Jasmine said after a moment.

"They can. It has saved people in this very kingdom, and neighboring ones, too."

"Do you have any left?"

"Wish I did, Princess. Used to have reserves for months and months, but with their low production lately it's all gone now."

"I see." Jasmine looked disappointed. "I had hoped that perhaps if you had any to spare it might be able to help Maha's little Usman."

"We'd tried the honey with him before," Maha said. "When he was a baby and the first fever struck we went to her straightaway. Zaria was generous. Gave us a batch for free to try out, but it didn't do a thing. Thankfully the weather improved and his fevers went away, so it wasn't a problem after that."

"I remember your boy." The beekeeper nodded. "Sorry to see the fevers have struck him again. The honey doesn't work with the little ones for some reason. I've tried tweaking the properties over the years but can't get it to work."

"How old is your son now?" Jasmine asked.

"Five days shy of three years old."

"Could the honey help a child that old?"

"Possibly." Zaria looked over at the boy. "It's worked for children a bit older than him. It would have been worth a try, had I any honey to give him."

Aladdin glanced at Jasmine; she looked deep in thought.

"Maha, you said you make awnings?" Jasmine finally said. "And Zaria, you said the trees losing their leaves is why your bees are suffering more this year, correct?"

"Yes." Zaria nodded. "But awnings won't help the bees. They are very particular about the olive tree's leaves providing shade."

"What if the awnings looked like the leaves of the olive trees? What if Maha could make awnings in the same shape as those leaves? Green fabric and all? Is that possible?" Jasmine looked at Maha.

"I could make it, yes." Maha nodded. "Never made leaflike awnings before, of course, but I have done more unusual designs than that. I have some firm wires I can use to attach them to the trunk—I could at least give it a try."

"Might work for a short while, at least," Zaria said slowly. She smiled for the first time. "Worth a shot, anyway."

"And if the bees had their shade . . ." Jasmine said.

"They could make honey for Usman," Aladdin said excitedly.

"They can make honey again in a matter of days if they're secure." Zaria nodded. "I don't know for sure if it can help your boy, and we'd need to see how the bees would react to the artificial shade, but maybe—just maybe—it could work." She turned to Maha. "We can hope, can't we?"

"Hope is more than what I came in with." Maha's eyes welled with tears. "Thank you, Prince Ali and Princess Jasmine. Thank you both for your help."

"Of course," Jasmine said. "I hope it works."

"Me too," Aladdin agreed.

Both of them were silent as they watched the women leave.

"That was such a simple solution," Aladdin said finally.

"Well, we don't know if it will work just yet."

"But still, it's something to try that hasn't been done before. And no one had thought about it until now."

"Sometimes, when you're so deeply involved in the pressures and the stress and your mind is so consumed by fear, you can miss easy solutions," Jasmine said.

At that moment, Omar approached them.

"We have one last person," he announced. "It's the man who came to the palace earlier. He put up such a fuss about being seen first that by the time he agreed to wait with the others, he ended up last in line. I will summon him now."

Aladdin looked at the paintings gracing the walls as Omar went to the door. The images of Ababwa. His kingdom. He and Jasmine were equals taking on the world together here. They sat in this very room and changed people's lives, working side by side. Back in Agrabah, both of their lives were difficult in different ways. Aladdin had to figure out where his next meal would come from, while Jasmine was stuck in a sort of gilded cage of her own. Though he knew Ababwa wasn't real, it would be as long as Jasmine and Aladdin remained here.

He wished they didn't have to leave at all. But, of course, he knew wishes were tricky things.

Jasmine

Chapter Nine

"*T*HE CARPET is still fast asleep, isn't it?" Jasmine observed. She leaned down and gently petted its soft fabric.

"Yep, looks all tuckered out, still." Ali looked affectionately at the magic rug. Then he turned to Jasmine. "Once this next person leaves, if you're still up for it, I'd love to show you the gardens and grounds."

"And the surprise?"

"Still remember that, huh?"

"As if I could forget," Jasmine laughed. She rested her back against the high-backed cushioned chair and thought back to all the people they'd met today. She didn't know if her idea would work for Zaria and Maha, but the two families thought they'd tried everything, and she'd given them one more chance to hope. She marveled at how easily Ali welcomed her advice and treated her as a peer. The more time she spent in Ababwa, the more she found herself falling for this charming little kingdom. And—she glanced at Ali—for him.

But before Jasmine could think upon this much more, her warm feelings disappeared as she saw the person walking into the Advisory Hall now.

It was *him*.

The man she'd glimpsed among the well-wishers when they had first arrived at the palace. The one who'd glared at them and made the hairs on the back of her neck tingle, just as they did now. She wondered what it was about this man that put her off as it did. Sure, he clearly wasn't as impressed as everyone else was with the prince. But unhappy subjects were part of the deal when it came to ruling a kingdom. It was more than that making Jasmine feel so uncomfortable. She frowned at his thin silvery hair—he was so familiar. It was almost as if she knew him, though she was completely certain they had never met before.

The man ambled up to the podium. Up close he was taller than he'd looked from afar. Scrawnier, too. His shirt was tattered and his hair was matted with dirt. Even from where he stood a fair distance away, Jasmine recognized the faint smell of salt water wafting over to them.

"Poor guy." Ali shook his head, whispering to Jasmine. "As much as I talk about how great Ababwa is, there's poverty here, too. He looks famished."

Jasmine watched the man examine a golden-framed painting along the wall. He craned his neck to study the vaulted ceilings, and then his eyes settled on the thrones. His eyes narrowed before he began coughing. Clearing the phlegm from this throat, he gripped the podium with his hands. He studied the two of them for a moment before speaking.

"Twenty-four karat?" he finally said. His voice was deep and gravelly.

"Excuse me?" asked Ali.

"That frame." The man nodded at the painting of

Ababwa he'd been studying. "They look to be solid gold. But surely they're just an imitation, aren't they?"

"They were here before my time," Ali said.

The man walked over to a frame and ran his hand across it.

"Well, it certainly feels as real as gold," he said, marveling.

"No one touches the property of the palace," Omar said firmly, marching over to the man.

"Easy there." The man raised an eyebrow. "Just admiring the premises is all. First time at this . . . what do you call it? Town hall meeting? My apologies to you," he said with a smirk. Jasmine wondered if Ali noticed the hostility that laced his words, but when she looked over at him, Ali wore a sympathetic expression instead.

"It's a big palace." Ali nodded. "I understand it can be a bit distracting."

"Big?" The man barked a laugh. "This isn't just big. This is the largest palace I've ever seen. Just how many people did it take to get this place up and running?"

"You know what they say." Ali laughed awkwardly. "It takes a kingdom."

"Takes *more* than a kingdom with this one." The man

snorted. "You some kind of wizard or magician or something? Because the way I—"

"If you have a question for the prince, a problem you need assistance with, please ask him now. Otherwise it is time for you to go," Omar said, interrupting him.

Doesn't he see that there is something off about this person? Jasmine wondered. She wanted to nudge Ali, but what could she say? The man was boorish, to be sure, but he hadn't actually done anything wrong. She simply had a bad feeling about him. And was that fair? She looked at the man now—he stared at their thrones as though he wished to inhale them.

"How can we help you?" Ali asked him.

"Help me?!" the man laughed. He ran a hand over his tattered clothing. "How does a person even begin to address all the problems I have?"

"New clothes?" Ali asked him. "We could start with that. Nothing wrong with what you're wearing, of course, but if you'd like we can get you some fresh outfits. Omar, can you please send for the palace tailor?"

"At once." Omar nodded and walked at a steady clip out of the hall.

The man watched Omar leave. He did not thank Ali. He seemed entirely indifferent, his arms crossed against his body. The three of them waited for a few moments in silence until Omar returned with the tailor in tow.

"Easy there," the man snarled when the woman bent down to measure his arms. "I'm not a mannequin you can just poke your pins into!"

"I haven't done anything but measure you with my tape," the tailor responded.

"Sorry," Ali said. "I know it must feel strange to get fitted for clothing, but I'm sure she will do a good job. When do you think it will be ready?" he asked her.

"I can have something put together by evening."

"That'll do," the man gruffly replied.

Just then, the magic carpet fluttered and stretched. It stuck a tassel up toward Jasmine before settling back down again.

The man's jaw dropped as he stared at it.

"That rug . . . It moved all on its own."

"Oh . . ." Ali reached down and smoothed out the carpet with his hand. "No, I don't think so. Probably a gust of wind that came through the opened door. So, your clothes," he said, quickly changing the subject. "Please do come back this evening, and we'll get you some food to go with it as well."

The man did not reply. Instead, he stared at the carpet. His eyes narrowed.

"If that is all . . ." Omar approached the man. "I can help show you the way out."

The man looked at Omar and then at both Jasmine and Ali before he turned and stalked out the door.

"That was strange," Ali said, watching him leave.

"Yes, it was," Jasmine agreed. She kept her eyes on the man as he stomped down the hallway and out the door. She waited until his figure had disappeared from view and breathed a sigh of relief once he was finally gone.

Aladdin

Chapter Ten

DONE WITH the open forum, Jasmine and Aladdin returned to the courtyard and stepped into the resplendent palace gardens. Flowers of every shape, size, and color bloomed around them. Sunflowers as tall as he was swayed in the distance. Tulips, poinsettias, and daffodils were spread throughout the grounds. Aladdin leaned down and brushed a hand against a patch of orchids to his left. They were as soft as silk.

"I'm not sure I've ever seen a tree sculpted into a flamingo before." Jasmine pointed to a shrub that did in fact look like a green flamingo, complete with a stick leg raised in midair.

"Me either," said Aladdin. "I mean, I've seen many other designs. I guess I never paid attention to this one before."

That was close. He was trying his best to act like trees sculpted into stars and birds and animals were ordinary for him, but it was difficult.

"I must admit you were right. This is a lovely surprise," she said.

"What is?"

"This." She gestured at the shrubbery. "The designs are very creative."

"You think *this* is the surprise? Wait until you see what it actually is." He pretended to be confident about the direction they were headed. Hopefully by following the paved walkway, the menagerie would pop up eventually.

"What on earth could be more fascinating than . . . wait a minute . . ." Her voice trailed off as they approached a white picket fence bordering a large expanse of land. "Is that . . ." She pointed to a red barnlike structure in the distance. "Is that a horse pen?"

"Looks like it," Aladdin said, relieved. The horses meant other animals had to be close. They walked over to the stable. There were at least twenty horses inside. Some were snow white, like the one in the foyer painting, but there were all sorts of colors, from black to chocolate brown to golden yellow.

Two chestnut horses approached them and nuzzled against Aladdin's hands.

"Hey there." Aladdin leaned down, pulled some orange carrots from a basket next to his feet, and proffered some. They inhaled the vegetables and rubbed their noses against him.

"Prince Ali." A freckled teenager, the stable hand, approached. He wore brown slacks and a yellow shirt. "Are you here to tour the menagerie?"

"Menagerie?" Jasmine repeated. She glanced toward the horizon and her eyes widened. "Is that a giraffe?"

"Surprise." Aladdin grinned.

"It's a fairly big place," the stable hand told the princess. "I can get saddles for these two horses so you can see as much as you can."

"Sounds great," Aladdin said.

The stable hand fitted both horses with saddles and then assisted Aladdin and Jasmine in mounting the steeds.

"Ready, friend?" Aladdin patted the horse's side once they were both seated. Holding on to the reins, together, Jasmine and Aladdin trotted deeper into the open field.

"Are those rhinos?" she asked incredulously after they had turned the bend past a thicket of trees. Sure enough, there was a family of four in the distance. Three of them were eating grass while one napped under a shade tree. "And ostriches?" She turned to her left. "And camels. And llamas and bears. Just how many animals do you have here?"

"A lot." Aladdin laughed.

"And those birds." Jasmine pointed to the sky at the pink birds with silver henna-like patterns. "They were the ones we saw when we first came to Ababwa. They were welcoming you because they live here! You didn't let on!"

"Well, it had to be a surprise," Aladdin said, thinking quickly.

"This is incredible," she said.

Yep, thought Aladdin. Genie had outdone himself

with this menagerie, and Aladdin could see Jasmine was enraptured by all of it.

An elephant calf that had been lounging with her parents by a mud patch near a pond waddled over to them now. Lifting her ridged gray trunk, she tickled Jasmine's feet. Jasmine laughed and leaned down to rub her ears before continuing on. The menagerie was filled with all sorts of other creatures, too: spider monkeys, peacocks, llamas, iguanas, even zebras. He hoped Jasmine didn't ask him to catalogue them all, because he would have no way to know just how many there were.

Farther out into a wide meadow, a cheetah approached, walking gracefully through a patch of tall grass.

"Is it dangerous?" she asked and glanced nervously at Aladdin. "I know I'm not one to talk what with Raja as my companion, but still . . ."

They watched from atop their horses as the cheetah approached until it was face to face with them. Then, to their surprise, it flopped down on its back.

"I think it wants a belly rub?" Aladdin said.

Dismounting, Jasmine bent down and petted the graceful creature. It let out a loud purr.

"I think she likes me!" Jasmine said.

"What's not to like?" Aladdin grinned.

Jasmine blushed and reached down again to pet the large cat's soft fur. Aladdin dismounted and gave it a quick ear rub.

"Raja loved when you did that," Jasmine said. "He's so protective over me. I don't think I've ever seen him warm up so quickly to anyone before."

"He's a pretty great tiger," Aladdin said. "Now if we could just find a way to bring him here, would there really be a reason to ever leave Ababwa?" He grinned at her. "How about it?"

Jasmine looked at him with a start. She hesitated, as though she were unsure how to respond.

"Oh, I was kidding," he said quickly. His cheeks flushed. "I didn't mean—"

"No, I mean, yes, I know you're joking," Jasmine said quickly. "Of course. But I guess I just . . . I wish it didn't have to end, either."

They trotted their horses back to the stable.

"Want to check out the streets of Ababwa?" he asked her as they dismounted. "Visit some of the shops and see the town up close?"

"I'd love that." She smiled.

They left the menagerie and headed toward the palace, talking about the town and the sights contained therein. But he couldn't shake one thought. Aladdin glanced at Jasmine. He'd been joking at first about moving to Ababwa, but now that he'd said it aloud, the thought wouldn't leave him. Why *did* their time here have to end? Why would anyone walk away from a place that was good and perfect and working for both of them to return to a place that wasn't?

Was it so ridiculous to wonder?

From *LEGENDARY LEADERS ACROSS THE AGES—*
"Princess Zeena, or: The Girl Who Traveled the World"

*T*HE PEOPLE of the kingdom of Saravania loved their verdant meadows with grazing goats and bright blue fireflies that glowed yellow against the evening sun. They loved how safe and secure they felt, their kingdom separated as it was from nearby lands by vast oceans.

"Beware the places beyond the sea," intoned teachers as children huddled close to one another. "Evil lurks beyond the horizon. People who harm and cause heartache and pain."

It wasn't that life was perfect on Saravania, for even in their kingdom there was a disease of late afflicting the pomegranate trees—and a rash of unexplained headaches and fevers afflicting the town elders. Still, even with that, life was good. They knew they were more fortunate than most, and of course they had their artwork. Be it stitch-work, painting, or ceramics, the people of Saravania were uncommonly gifted in the arts, and despite the imper-fections there may have been, everyone was grateful and content.

Everyone except Princess Zeena.

"It's really too much," the sultana, her mother, would admonish her. "You are a princess in a most beautiful kingdom, and yet you pout and sulk and are unsatisfied."

Zeena gazed out the window and said nothing. It was an argument with no proper resolution. Her younger sis-ters were gifted artists, stitching oceans from thread and painting fireflies that looked so lifelike one could think they were genuine. And though Zeena admired these pur-suits, they could not capture her heart completely.

Zeena often looked out at the deep blue waters from the window of her bedroom tower. Fishermen docked just a few feet from shore, not far from the royal sailboat;

their lines sank into the abyss. Seagulls swooped in the sky and dove into the water before flying on. She had grown up on the stories of the dangers beyond the horizon like everyone else, but if there were dangers, she wished to see them for herself. She wondered if other lands had palaces like their own. If they had festivals to celebrate the sun and the moon twice a year. What sorts of clothes did they wear? What languages did they speak? Did they laugh and smile differently from the people of Saravania? How similar were they to her? How different?

Zeena craved *different*. And she resented the uniformity of Saravania as much as everyone else seemed to find comfort in it. While others drew and painted, Zeena wandered to the shore behind her castle and searched the coves for undiscovered shells and treasures. And it was at such a moment that, one day, her destiny unfolded.

As she sat by a beachy cove one balmy summer afternoon, Zeena heard a loud splash. A fisherman's boat capsized before her eyes. The man's hands flailed about, the ocean's riptide so strong it threatened to carry him out to sea. Zeena leapt up and dove into the water. As she helped him to shore, the fisherman thanked her profusely for saving his life.

And then, Zeena had an idea.

The next day she approached the man as he prepared to board his boat.

"Would you have any idea how to operate a sailboat?" she asked him.

"Yes, Princess." The man nodded. "I'm proficient with most of the boats on our island."

"Could you teach me how our royal sailboat might work? And would I be able to count on your discretion?"

"You saved my life. Anything you ask for is yours," the man said.

As the weeks passed, the man taught Zeena the workings of a sailboat. How the mast flew up and blew out, how to stop it in rough waters to keep from capsizing, and the ways to change its direction based on how the wind blew.

When the sultana walked in later that week to find Zeena stitching red thread onto a white cloth at her desk, she startled.

"What is this?" she asked her daughter.

"Embroidery," Zeena said, too consumed with her work to even glance up. "The family emblem, for our royal sailboat. I thought it would be nice to have a new look for it."

"That's a marvelous idea." The sultana could have danced for joy seeing her daughter absorbed as she was with her work. "We can display it at the festival, perhaps," her mother said.

"I don't know if it will be done by then," Zeena said thoughtfully.

"Take your time. Art requires the utmost patience." Her mother squeezed her shoulder and then walked away.

Day after day Zeena worked on the embroidery. Soon brilliant flowers bloomed all along the cloth. Everyone agreed it was the most beautiful sail they'd ever seen.

The day of the festival, Zeena began to cough.

"Are you sick?" her younger sister asked her.

"I am." Zeena sneezed. Looking at her sister's concerned expression, she felt a sharp pang of guilt, but she also knew she had to carry out her plan to control her own destiny.

She waved goodbye to her family as they left for the festivities, promising to join them later if she improved over the day. As soon as the palace was empty—for the holiday meant everyone had the day off—Zeena hopped out of bed, grabbed the embroidered sail and her knapsack filled with supplies for her journey, and quietly slipped out.

When the sun began to set and the sultana and her other daughters returned, they discovered Zeena was missing. No one worried at first. Danger simply did not visit their island, and Zeena loved finding new hideaways; she would return soon enough. But as night deepened with no trace of her, worry grew. Just as the sultana was about to call for the servants to scour the beaches, she heard a scream.

Her youngest daughter pointed out the window. The sailboat was missing from its dock.

A tear rolled down the sultana's face. Her eldest had chosen to go beyond the horizon. With no sign of the boat to be seen, there was nothing to be done about it now.

• ► • ◄ •

As the months passed with no sign of her, even those who had held on to hope—who thought perhaps Zeena would defy the odds—realized she would not return. And life had grown increasingly difficult on Saravania. The crop disease, once confined to the pomegranate trees, had spread, swift as a fire. The date, fig, and olive trees were destroyed. The grapes, all brown and dried, hung limp from their vines. And the headaches and fevers that once afflicted only a handful of the town's elders now spread to more and more people. It was as though, with Zeena's departure, a gray cloud had settled over their small kingdom, never to lift again.

Until the day she returned.

It was her youngest sister who saw her first, the white sail of the family boat a speck in the distance glimmering brighter and brighter as it grew closer. News spread quickly and soon every last person in the kingdom stood upon the shore to watch a miracle unfold. Zeena was back—and not only was she definitively not dead, but her skin was a deep golden brown, her hair was kissed by the sun, and she wore a large smile upon her face.

After embracing her mother and sisters and greeting the townspeople, all of whom were too relieved to see her alive to be angry, she listened to the troubles that had befallen the island in her absence.

But as they spoke, Zeena simply smiled.

"What is there to be happy about?" the sultana asked, unable to hide her irritation.

"I'm sorry, Mother," Zeena said. "I only smiled because I believe I can help."

She went to the boat and returned with a sack, drawing from it a packet of seeds—green and so tiny that one had to squint to truly get the measure of them. The townspeople followed her as she sprinkled them over a field of pomegranate trees. She did the same at the next parcel of land, continuing until she had scattered the green seeds on every plot of vegetation.

"What are you doing?" asked a child looking on as she spread the last of them. But before she could reply, the villagers startled, for they could have sworn the trees and plants stood straighter than before.

"The disease on our crops isn't unique to Saravania," Zeena explained. "Many other lands have this same affliction. These seeds were discovered to reverse the disease and restore the leaves, stems, and roots to health. And speaking of health"—Zeena turned to the people—"I learned that there are many things on our own island kingdom that contain powers we did not know."

She showed them how the leaves of the Maza trees

that bloomed with pink and yellow flowers around the island, once ground into water, could reduce any fever in seconds. She plucked the roots of the Sigma berry and explained how, when boiled, they could cure any headache.

"There's more as well," Zeena promised. "But these will help us to begin to heal what is broken on Saravania."

"So, the other kingdoms. It isn't frightening out there?" her younger sister asked her.

"It can be," Zeena told her. "I *have* met some awful people during my travels. There was one land where a rich man burned nearly half his kingdom for greed, but there were many more good people—people we have a lot to learn from."

As the days passed, the crops began to heal. Within weeks the grapevines and the trees of figs, dates, and olives bloomed again, more plentiful than ever. The illnesses, too, began to abate.

"You saved our kingdom," Zeena's mother said. "You were brave and intuitive enough to know we needed to look beyond our borders. I was too shortsighted to see. It is you, my child, who should be queen." The sultana moved to remove her crown, but Zeena interceded.

"I do not wish to be sultana," Zeena told her mother gently. "Saravania is lucky to have you. I simply wish to continue my work. The world should know how we live; our beautiful artwork deserves wider recognition, and we can learn so much from others."

From that day forward, with the queen's blessings, upon a newly built ship and with a small crew, Zeena continued her journeys. She traveled to nearly every kingdom, touched upon every continent, and returned home every few months to share her knowledge and the partnerships she had built and to collect more works from the gifted artisans of the island to sell in the lands beyond. And from then on, the kingdom of Saravania was no longer hidden from the world, but a part of it.

Jasmine

Chapter Eleven

"WE'RE HEADING OUT for a walk around the main city center of Ababwa," Ali told Omar when they walked back into the foyer.

"Shall I call for the carriage?" Omar asked as the magic carpet zipped over to them.

"No carriage ride. I'd love to walk," Jasmine said. "It's the best way to take in the sights, I think."

The carpet drooped at this.

"Oh, did you want to take us around? Sorry," she told the carpet gently. "It's just that we wanted to pop into shops and look around a bit. It'll be easier on foot, I think."

"Why don't you stay here and relax?" Ali said. "We'll be back soon enough."

The magic carpet flew over to the foot of the sofa and stretched out on the floor.

Together, Ali and Jasmine stepped out through the palace doors. The guards, standing at attention in their navy and silver regalia, saluted them as they approached and wordlessly parted the wrought iron gates. Turning down the street, Jasmine glanced back at the palace walls. "Is this okay? Us just walking out and about, without any guards for protection?"

"Oh, yeah, guards . . ." Ali glanced back. "Ababwa is safe. We'll be okay."

While the palace was a gaudy display of wealth, there was no denying the charm that bounced off the walls in the streets of Ababwa. And the way the sun hung low in the sky right now and hit the cobblestoned roads, it felt as though the entire town were coated in a marvelous, glittering sheen. Thanks to the sloping terrain of Ababwa, Jasmine could see beyond the roads to the grassy gardens and trees behind them, as well as the curved cliffs in the distance.

"Are those steps carved into the cliff?" Jasmine squinted.

"Maybe." Ali peered with a hand over his eyes. "I think so. Yes."

"Never been?"

He shook his head. "It's not the biggest kingdom, but there are still parts I haven't explored yet."

The homes they passed now were modest ones but well-kept, with brilliant red, orange, and patterned curtains covering windows. Some were thrown open to the fresh air, curtains swaying in the breeze.

"It's quiet out here," Jasmine observed. "After seeing all the people lined up to greet us when we first arrived, I expected things to be much busier."

"They'll probably be out and about in the town square this time of day," he told her. "It should be just a little further up."

"Is that where the huge fountain was?" she asked. "I think I saw people carrying buckets to it."

"Yes." He smiled. His eyes lit up at this.

"They can get water at any time without charge?"

"I think it's important for people to be able to have water to provide for themselves and their families. Water is something no one should have to worry about."

"We should do that in Agrabah," Jasmine said. "I think that—"

Suddenly, Ali's hand shot up in front of her.

"What's the matter?" She looked up at him—his expression was tense, his body taut like a coiled spring.

"The noise." Ali glanced about. "You didn't hear it?"

"No." She craned her neck and turned to look around: "I don't see a soul."

"Sorry," he said, but he remained alert, standing still. "I just . . . I thought I saw something. Heard someone . . ."

"What sort of noise did you hear?"

"Nothing." He slowly relaxed. "It was nothing. Just in my head, I guess."

Jasmine looked at him curiously for a moment before they continued on.

•►•◄•

That was close, the man thought. He breathed a sigh of relief and wiped away the sweat on his brow from where he stood huddled in the narrow brick alleyway. He'd only taken a few steps toward them before he'd kicked that pebble against the cobblestoned road, inadvertently drawing attention to himself.

The boy is quick. No doubt about it, thought the man. But the boy did not notice the man now as he stepped out of the alleyway and watched their dwindling figures. The man narrowed his eyes. He glanced back at the palace in the distance, calculating his next move.

• ► ◄ •

Shops began to crop up on either side of Jasmine and Ali as the pair walked toward the town square. It certainly was a different experience to stroll the streets of Ababwa on foot as compared to watching it all pass by from a carriage. As Ali had predicted, the streets grew noisier now with people hurrying in and out of shops. Some carried sacks with loaves of bread poking out from the tops, while others held the hands of small children firmly in their own.

Jasmine was surprised people weren't mobbing them. They had been so excited to see them when they first arrived. But it also made sense. If you treated people with dignity and respect—and if you gave them forums to freely approach and discuss their issues so they felt heard and understood—they would treat you with respect as well.

"You're fast on your feet, aren't you?" Jasmine said as they walked.

"What do you mean?"

"Just back then, earlier, when we were walking over here, you were so relaxed and comfortable one minute, and then you changed in an instant, literally on your toes, ready to do whatever it was you thought you needed to do."

"Yeah," Ali said. "I guess all that princely training over the years helped with my athletic abilities."

But it wasn't just athletic abilities, Jasmine thought. Ali had a particular instinct. A kind of street smart she never had expected to find in a royal prince.

"Oh!" Ali smacked his forehead with his hand. "I almost forgot!"

"What?"

"A place I need to show you. It's probably by the town square."

"What is it?"

"It's a surprise."

"You sure love surprises." She rolled her eyes.

"I love them just as much as you hate them." He laughed. "But you have to admit that the last one was worth the wait, wasn't it?"

Well, she thought with a smile, *that is indeed true.*

Jasmine looked around and wondered where he was taking her. With the interesting topography of this kingdom, there were probably untold hidden lagoons and romantic overlooks. Ali stopped at a nondescript storefront and poked his head in.

"Yep." He nodded. "This is the place. We're here!"

"Here?" Jasmine looked at the creaky door.

Well, Ali was right. She *was* surprised.

It took a moment for her eyes to adjust once she had stepped into the modest shop lit by lanterns hanging from the rafters.

"Welcome," said a man with round metal spectacles. He approached them with a broad smile. He was bald and had a gray mustache. "My name is Ahmed. Please make yourself at home and feel free to look around at anything you'd like."

And that's when Jasmine's eyes adjusted enough

to understand where they were. This was a *cartography shop*. She spun around and saw that all four walls were lined with beautiful, intricate maps. Some were painted vibrant colors—works of art in their own right—while others showed practical gray outlines of countries, cities, and continents. There were black-and-white maps outlining local boundaries. And world maps. There were crisp new ones folded in rectangles on the table before them and old ones in opened wooden drawers, their edges worn and frayed like those of the maps she had back home. A set of globes rested on a bookshelf on the other end of the wall.

"I can't believe it," she said. "I'm not sure I've ever seen a shop dedicated exclusively to maps like this before."

"We have books, too, if those interest you at all." Ahmed pointed to a section of small bookshelves against the far wall. Their spines indicated the history of the world, the oceans beneath their feet, and the sky above.

Jasmine walked over to an array of maps spread across a large table. One was titled *The Greatest Kingdoms on Earth*. Another one mapped out the countries with the most exotic animals. Her eyes landed then on a map with a faded legend. She glanced at the shop owner. "Sir,

I was wondering if I could look at this one. It looks old, so I understand if it's best I don't."

"Oh, please, call me Ahmed. And yes, of course, Princess. You're welcome to browse anything you'd like."

Jasmine lost herself among the shelves and tables of maps. She pored over the different legends, the tiny details of mountain ranges and paths of rivers and lakes. How different so many were from the ones she had at home! She had presumed the maps she had collected over the years were the only standard type, but there appeared now to be all sorts of ways to record the same information. There was even an entire book on the art of cartography. She could easily have stayed in this shop all day. She trailed her hands over an ancient map and saw how the borders of the world had changed and flowed over the years.

"Good surprise?" Ali asked. She looked at his boyish smile—the look of nervousness that had suddenly returned.

"I don't know what to say," she said, looking around. "It's as if this store was made especially for me. It's . . . it's perfect."

"I'm so glad you like it."

She looked up at Ali. In just the short time they'd known each other, he knew the perfect place to take her. He understood her in a way no one else in her life did.

Jasmine reached up and hugged him. She saw his look of surprise when she leaned toward him and felt the way he melted into her embrace. She pulled back and met his gaze. His eyes were on hers; he was so close to her. His breath was sweet and warm. Were it not for Ahmed, politely busying himself not far from them and pretending not to notice, she would have kissed him right then and there.

"I don't know if anyone has ever done anything this thoughtful for me before," she said shyly. "Thank you for this. For bringing me here."

"My pleasure, Princess," Ali said, gazing intently at her.

• ► ◄ •

The sun hung lower in the sky when they at last stepped out into the town square. Jasmine looked around at the stalls lining the square courtyard; they were not unlike the ones they had back home in Agrabah. A woman sold jewelry in one stall. Another had scarves in red, green, and pink, tied to the stall and flowing in the breeze. A leather maker showed off woven belts and wallets, and another seller displayed wood-carved flutes and walking sticks.

"This looks interesting," Ali remarked as he approached a table with a medley of things from pens to candles to dress purses.

Jasmine picked up a tiny coin purse but frowned when her hands ran over it.

"Is this . . ." She picked it up and examined it closely. "Is this a cookie?"

"It is, Princess." The vendor, a woman with glasses on the ridge of her nose, beamed proudly. "Designed all of these creations from flour, sugar, and a little butter right in my kitchen. With a little baking magic, I can make just about any sweet look like anything else. I do custom orders as well. Please try one!"

Jasmine watched as Ali decided which one to taste. She took in his dimple. The way his hair fluttered in the gentle breeze. It was uncanny how much he reminded her of the boy she had met at the marketplace. Maybe he had family in Agrabah? Jasmine wondered. She was about to ask him about this when a woman's voice called out to them.

"Princess Jasmine! Prince Ali!"

Zaria, the beekeeper, approached them. Her gilded cage of bees hung from her arm, but instead of the tense expression she'd worn earlier, she was smiling.

"Just came back from Maha's home," the woman told them. "She drew up a few sketches, and I think the awning really will resemble the canopy they miss! At least real enough to do for now. We're going to test a few out tonight to see if the bees will accept it. And if the bees *can* make honey, we'll give some to the boy. He's older now. It may work."

"That's excellent news!" Ali said.

"I hope this will put your worries at ease," Jasmine said.

"I'm the last in the line for this trade. Broke my heart when I thought it would all end with me."

They talked for a bit longer before Zaria walked away. Now that she'd actually helped people and seen the effect her advice could have, Jasmine didn't know how she could bear to go back to Agrabah and be once again a girl in a gilded cage, not unlike the bees Zaria swung from her arm.

She glanced over at Ali, who was chatting with the dessert vendor. How easily he had invited her to sit with him at the advisory council. How completely he trusted her and turned to her for advice. How thoughtful he was to take her to the map shop. The menagerie.

Until this trip to Ababwa, the prospect of spending her life with another person had seemed as abhorrent as dipping her hand in a hornet's nest. Marriage was on her father's agenda, not hers. She thought of how Ali had joked about their staying here forever. And though she didn't yet know if she wanted to marry Prince Ali, the idea of living here with someone who shared her sense of adventure, who was funny and kind, and who treated her as an equal—and of actually making a *difference* in a kingdom rather than simply dreaming about it from her living quarters—sounded more and more enticing with each passing moment.

Something tugged at her hands just then.

Looking down, she saw an empty palm; the coin-purse cookie was gone.

A little boy raced off toward the other side of the town square.

"Hey!" shouted the vendor, her cheeks flushed pink with anger. Instantly, half the townspeople in the square gave chase after the boy.

"Stop!" Jasmine shouted at them, but she was drowned out by the sounds of the angry pursuers.

Jasmine and Ali took off, rushing to keep up with the others until at last everyone came to a halt. Slipping through the crowd, they reached the front and saw the boy cornered against a brick storefront wall. He was younger than she'd first thought. He couldn't have been more than eight or nine years old. His dark hair stuck out awkwardly at all different angles, and his clothes were at least two sizes too small and worn at the knees and elbows. His green eyes looked at the crowd with fear. The cookie was clenched in his hand, bits of it crumbling to the ground.

"Now you've really done it," a man said, glowering.

"You steal from us all the time, but stealing from a princess?" shouted another.

"Princess?" The boy's eyes widened. The cookie fell to the ground; his hands went limp at his sides. "I'm s-s-sorry," the boy stuttered. "I d-d-didn't know."

"It's only a cookie," Jasmine said gently.

"Yes, but he didn't know that!" said the man at the front of the crowd. His face was beet red. "Thought it was an actual coin purse, didn't you?" He sneered. The boy blushed and the man barked out a laugh. "That's what I figured. Now the prince will find a punishment suitable for the likes of you once and for all."

"Wait!" Ali squeezed through the crowd and hurried over to the boy.

"He's just a child." Zaria turned to Ali. "Please have mercy on him, Your Majesty."

"What does his being young have to do with this?" the man asked. "Sneaks food out of my shop nearly every day of the week!"

"Took the bread I had left out to cool just this morning," added a baker with a nod.

The voices shouted over one another, blending into a cacophonous roar of accusations.

"Enough!" Ali shouted.

In an instant, the square grew silent. The boy looked at both Ali and Jasmine. His eyes glistened with tears. Ali walked up to the boy and leaned down. Placing a hand on the boy's shoulder, he studied him; his expression grew somber.

"The boy did something wrong," Ali finally said, turning to address the crowd. "But it was a mistake."

"Respectfully, Your Majesty," the man said, "his stealing from the princess was no mistake."

"Well, it is me he took from, and so this matter is between me and him," Jasmine interjected.

"What's your name?" Ali asked the boy.

"Jamaal," the boy whispered.

"That's a nice name," he said. "It means beauty, doesn't it?"

Jamaal shrugged. He looked down at the cookie on the ground, leaned down, and picked it up.

"It's dirty now," he said, turning it over in his hands. "I'm sorry I stole it. I didn't think it was a coin purse. I knew it was a cookie, and I get hungry sometimes, and when I get hungry I don't think much about what I'm doing. I just want to eat and I can't think about much else. I don't have any money. Or I'd buy you a new one, Princess."

"Don't worry about that," she said. "Do you live around here?"

"Not far."

"Let us walk you home," Ali said. "Your parents must be worried about where you've run off to."

"He doesn't have parents," Zaria said. "Died last year.

That's the tragedy of it all. Growing up on the streets means he gets by however he can."

"Oh . . ." Ali's voice trailed off.

"We've been generous." The baker crossed his arms defensively. "We don't let the boy go hungry. We give him food and mend his clothes if he'll sit still long enough to let us. But we've got our own worries, too. And he doesn't ask. He simply takes."

"Maybe he could do better about asking," Ali said. "But he's just a boy. Weren't you all little once? We could do worse than being patient with a child in need. Perhaps his actions are vexing, but compassion is what defines our humanity, doesn't it?"

"You are right, Prince Ali," the man said after a moment, sighing. He looked a bit abashed now. The crowd murmured to one another and then, the confrontation over, they began to disperse.

"Thank you for forgiving me," Jamaal said. "I will repay you for the cookie. I promise I will try my best."

"There's no debt," Jasmine said.

"That's right," Ali said. "Come with us."

They walked over to the stall of treats and Ali paid the woman, letting the boy choose his favorites. Jamaal's eyes widened as he took in the cat, puppy, and goldfish creations, but he barely looked them over before he ate them all.

"Easy there," Ali laughed. "There's more where those came from."

They walked over to a corn stall and bought him buttered corn sprinkled with black peppers, and then a pita stuffed with cabbage, seasoned pickles, and roasted chicken. The boy devoured all of it.

Ali studied the boy as he finished off the last of a bag of candied almonds they'd purchased.

"I was thinking," Ali said. "Why don't you come back to the palace with me? I have plenty of extra bedrooms. You can pick whichever one you like."

"No, thank you," Jamaal said. His cheeks grew crimson. "What you've done for me is more than enough."

"But you could work for me in exchange for room and board and all the food you can eat. What do you think?"

The boy studied the ground.

"Fine." Ali reached into his satchel and pulled out a handful of gold coins. "Take some to tide you over while you think about it?"

Jamaal stared at the money and then at both Princess Jasmine and Ali. He snatched the money from Ali's palm and hurried away.

"Wait!" Jasmine called out. But the boy didn't stop. He rushed out of the square, turned the corner, and disappeared from view.

"No use chasing him," Ali said quietly. "He won't come with us if he doesn't want to."

"Even with that money, he needs some supervision and guidance. A child that young shouldn't be on his own." Jasmine shook her head. "We could at least try to find him. Surely people around here know where he lives."

"It wouldn't work. I know kids like him. They have a hard time trusting because they've been let down too many times. Even if we found him and took him to the palace, he'd find a way to escape. He probably knows the streets better than anyone else." He looked at Jasmine. "What we need in Ababwa is a place for boys like him. It's like you said earlier about free clinics for people who can't afford it. Children like Jamaal should be protected by the kingdom they live in—they deserve a bed to sleep in and food to eat without having to rely on the kindness of strangers."

"An orphanage." She nodded. "No child should have to worry about their next meal."

"Losing a parent is hard enough."

Jasmine looked at Ali. He looked heartbroken by the boy's plight.

She could do worse, she knew, than spending a lifetime with a person like Ali—who cared not just for her, but for all his people, including those who had the least.

Aladdin

Chapter Twelve

THE SKY was ablaze with violet, pink, and navy blue streaks trailing above like a painted canvas. Aladdin felt a tinge of sadness. Soon the darkness would overtake all the light around them and coat the sky completely.

"It's getting dark," Jasmine observed. "Are you sure it's not getting too late?"

"We still have some time to explore, if you're okay with that."

"More than okay." Jasmine smiled.

Aladdin remembered the restaurant he'd asked Genie to re-create for him in Ababwa, his favorite hole-in-the-wall back in Agrabah. They couldn't leave without trying it—it was one of the few things in this kingdom that contained a part of who he truly was.

"Care for a bite at one of my favorite dessert shops?" asked Aladdin. "There's a great place I love that shouldn't be too far from here."

"If it's a favorite of yours, how can I say no?"

"You won't regret it," he promised. "They make the best sweets and teas you've ever had."

Had it not been for the familiar scent of Bilal's sweet cheese pastries wafting through the shop window, Aladdin would never have been able to find the place. The version of the café that Genie had created for Ababwa was unrecognizable. Stepping inside, Aladdin took in the charming open-air restaurant with cushioned floor seating, low wooden tables, and glass lanterns hanging from the ceiling above. Aladdin tried to keep from laughing. He'd have to let Genie know next time he saw him that he'd done an incredible job indeed.

The store owner walked over and welcomed them. He looked like the same one from back in Agrabah, but instead of the grease- and flour-spattered apron and perpetual frown the man back home always wore, this Bilal had starched cream clothing and grinned from ear to ear. It was a most peculiar sight.

"Please sit anywhere you'd like," the man said, gesturing to the tables. "Shall I bring the usual desserts along with a menu?"

"Sounds great." Aladdin settled down across from Jasmine on a red cushioned seat by a large open window overlooking the street outside. Music wafted over to them now from somewhere in the distance.

"Oh, wow," Jasmine said when the owner returned carrying an oversized wooden tray filled to the edges with small porcelain plates of food. There was indeed every plump pastry, chocolate, and kunafa Aladdin had ever seen at the original spot back home piled onto the tray, along with a pot of tea and Aladdin's favorite lemon drink. Unlike in Agrabah, where the desserts were served on napkins and the teas and juices handed to customers in drab metal tins, here the tea was steeped in rose-pink pots with cups and saucers set before them. Aladdin's tall, cool glass of lemonade was handed to him in a crystal glass.

"There's no way I can eat all of this," Jasmine said, taking in the feast before them.

"We can give it our best shot?" Aladdin grinned.

Jasmine ate a forkful of honey-glazed pastry. "Now *this* is what I call dessert."

A group of children danced past them just outside the shop. The eldest of the bunch beat drums, and the rest skipped along the walkway. They didn't notice Jasmine and Aladdin watching, immersed as they were in one another and the music. The kids were truly and fully happy. And right now, sitting across from Jasmine, that was how Aladdin felt, too. Ababwa was not perfect, that much was certain—what with that man who'd come to see him in tattered clothing, and Jamaal, who wandered the streets alone—but at least here Aladdin could *do* something about what was wrong instead of simply simmering at the injustice of it all. If there was a problem in Ababwa, *he* could fix it. Maybe the land wasn't technically real, but did that matter? It was real right now.

And then there was Jasmine. He gazed at her now. She was kind, warm, wise, and fiercely intelligent. And even if she didn't love surprises, she loved exploring and adventures just as he did. He glanced down at her hand, resting just inches from his own, and clasped his hand over hers. The warmth sent a shot of lightning to his heart. There was no denying that Jasmine was absolutely perfect for him, and it didn't matter if he'd known her for a few minutes or for a lifetime. He realized in this moment . . . that he loved her.

And there was also no denying that she was a princess. And once they left Ababwa, he would no longer have a kingdom.

Heaviness settled over his heart as the sky turned darker outside. Their time here was nearing its end.

But did it have to?

Maybe, just maybe, she'd take a chance on him. On them. He'd joked about it earlier, but maybe he could tell her now exactly how he felt—and ask her to stay with him here. After all, Ababwa would remain the kingdom it appeared to be so long as they both stayed. All he had to do was figure out a way to bring Abu here, and to get Raja for Jasmine, and everything would be all set. He was about to say just this when Jasmine spoke.

"I can't stop thinking about that poor boy," Jasmine said. "Can you imagine what it's like to not only lose your parents but also have no one at all to watch out for you?"

So there it was. Aladdin's throat tightened. He didn't need to imagine how Jamaal felt, because *he* was that boy. Sure, Genie had given Jamaal green eyes instead of Aladdin's dark brown, but Aladdin recognized himself in the boy all the same.

And he couldn't tell Jasmine.

As honest as she was with him, he couldn't be honest with her. Not fully.

"How are you finding everything?" The shop owner approached them now. His hands were clasped in front of him.

"Fantastic," Jasmine told him. "The honey-glazed pastry was my favorite."

"I can prepare another for you if you'd like."

"Oh." Jasmine glanced at Aladdin. "I probably shouldn't. . . ."

"Well, it's not every day you come to Ababwa, is it?" the shop owner insisted.

Jasmine thanked the man and Aladdin watched the chipper shop owner head back toward the kitchen. Just then, he caught sight of another man inside the shop. And the glint of a bag, fluttering in the air. The man hurried out of the restaurant. Where had he come from?

Aladdin wondered. But then his blood went cold as he took a closer look at the satchel the man gripped in his hands. The gray cloth. The gold string. It was the same one filled with coins—and, more importantly, the *lamp*—that Aladdin had worn at his waist.

"Hey!" Aladdin jumped up in an instant.

"What's wrong?" Jasmine asked.

But Aladdin had already leapt out of the open window, giving full chase.

"Stop!" Aladdin shouted after the man.

But the man hurried on at a quick pace. Aladdin ran as fast as he could until he caught up. He yanked the man roughly by the arm. If the man had the lamp, all of this—Ababwa, Ali—could be undone in a matter of seconds.

"Get your hands off of me!" the man yelled before turning around. But once he saw who it was, his hands dropped to his sides and his face grew pale. "Prince Ali!" he cried. He was a short man; a bit of gray peppered his hair and beard. "I apologize for my rudeness. I did not realize it was you. What can I do for you, Your Majesty?"

"Are you honestly going to pretend you didn't just steal from me?"

"Steal from you?" the man gasped. "Never, sir!"

"How can you say that so confidently?" Aladdin stared at the man. "You're holding my satchel in your hands right now and lying?"

The man stared at the satchel and yelped. It fell to the ground.

"I don't understand it." Aladdin picked up the satchel. "To take from me like this?"

"I am so sorry." The man's voice trembled. "Please forgive me."

"You could have simply asked me if you needed money," Aladdin continued. Jasmine had caught up to them now. "I would have helped you. . . ." His voice trailed off when he opened the satchel. He ran his hand through it to be sure. There was no lamp, no gold coins in the satchel. Instead he pulled out work tools. Screws, nails, a small hammer.

"But this makes no sense," Aladdin murmured. He looked down at his waist . . . and saw that his satchel was tied exactly as it had been.

Glancing around now, he saw that many of the men walking past wore similar satchels with the same gold ties. How could he not have noticed that before?

"I'm so sorry," the man repeated. "I was fixing the furnace of Bilal's restaurant. It's always breaking down for one reason or other, as you know, and I'm the only one who knows how to get it work just right. I was rushing out the door to get back to my wife; I'm late for a wedding. I'd lost track of time. So I ran. But that's no excuse. Forgive me for taking what belonged to you."

"Forgive you?" Aladdin's head throbbed. Why did this man not defend himself? Why did he accept the blame when he wasn't at fault? He handed the man back his satchel. "This satchel doesn't belong to me. I was mistaken. I should apologize to you. I hope *you* will forgive me."

The man shrank from the satchel Aladdin proffered. "It's yours, Prince."

"No," Aladdin said. "It's not." He placed the satchel back in the man's hands. "I don't understand. You only had to tell me what was in the bag. That you hadn't stolen it."

"And contradict the prince of Ababwa?" The man's voice sounded incredulous. "I would never do such a thing. I am forever indebted to you for all you have done for our kingdom. The battle of Amad? The way you strategically sent in forces to save our homes from destruction?

And who could ever forget the hunger years? The way you gave to your kingdom of your own belongings, distributing fairly so not a soul went hungry? You have saved our lives and our livelihoods countless times from destruction and peril. This entire kingdom, including myself, is indebted to you."

But I haven't done any of those things, Aladdin thought. He watched the man retreat into the distance, still uttering words of apology.

For the first time since they'd arrived in Ababwa, the reality of this kingdom finally settled in to him.

This kingdom.

It didn't exist.

It was fabricated.

All the conquests this man loved him for had never happened. All these people who adored him and had lined the streets upon their arrival . . . what had he actually done to deserve their affection?

Nothing.

"It's okay." He felt the soft touch of a hand on his arm. Jasmine looked at him, her expression filled with concern.

"I humiliated a man old enough to be my father," Aladdin said. "All because I assumed he was stealing from me. I didn't even pause to think it through."

"You acted on instinct. You didn't know."

"That was awful."

"It wasn't your greatest moment," Jasmine conceded. "But mistakes are part of being human. History is full of kings and princes and viziers who make mistakes but never own up to them. You apologized to the man. You took responsibility. He knows your heart, and he knows all you've done for this kingdom. You've been a good leader for your kingdom, and he respected that."

But I haven't *been a good leader,* Aladdin thought. *I am no leader at all.* He could still see the look of fear in that man's eyes. He knew that look. How many times had he been on the other end of such a false accusation? He knew the way it twisted at your heart like stalks of poison and how it eventually made you question your own worth.

Jasmine could tell him that he shouldn't feel too bad, but it was only because she didn't know the truth. She thought the man's stories were true and that Aladdin had done all the great feats that the man spoke of with admiration. She did not know that none of these people truly loved him, because none of them was real.

The one thing Aladdin wanted more than anything was to be somebody worthwhile, but this wasn't the way to do it. He looked at Jasmine, her arms crossed, watching him with a worried expression. Unlike himself, the princess who stood before him was the real deal. A leader who had spent her life studying and training and doing everything she could, even with her restrictive circumstances, to be someone who could lead someday.

And she deserved to lead *real* people whose lives she could truly and genuinely impact. As for Aladdin? He knew he wanted to be worthy of her admiration and respect, but he wanted to earn her love by being the man she thought he was.

And how could he do that in a kingdom built on a lie?

Jasmine

Chapter Thirteen

JASMINE AND ALI walked toward the palace down the cobblestoned street. The sun was all but gone now; street lanterns along the way lent a colorful glow to the city. Neither of them said it aloud just yet, but they both knew it was about time to leave.

She glanced over at Ali. Ever since the misunderstanding with the mechanic from the restaurant, he'd grown quieter. She could see by his expression how the guilt still clawed away at him. Jasmine wished she could say something to ease his conscience, but she also knew that as much as she might like to help him feel better, this was probably something he'd need to wrestle with on his own. She still couldn't get over how nimbly he'd leapt out the window to run after the man—those were instincts she'd seen once before. The similarities continued to gnaw at her. Was she trying to force a connection between Ali and Aladdin that wasn't there? Or was there something to her suspicions?

"I was thinking," Ali said just then as they walked past a meadow. "Remember those stone steps we saw earlier by the cliffs? They're right here. Want to check out what's down there before we leave? Just one last stop . . ."

"One last stop," she echoed. What would be the harm? "I'd love that.

"Those steps are safe?" she asked once they reached them. Up close they were steep and sculpted right into the cliffside.

"They look pretty sturdy," he said. He got onto the first one and jumped down a step. "See? I know it's dark, though. If you don't feel safe, we won't go down."

"It's bright enough with the moon. What's down there exactly?"

"Well, it's a—"

"Surprise," she finished. "You and the surprises."

"This one will be a surprise for both of us," Ali said. "But I think it should be pretty nice, and my surprises have been worth it so far, haven't they?"

"They have," she agreed.

The steps were indeed large and sturdy, and despite how steep the cliff was, Jasmine was surprised how securely they made their way down.

She gasped when they took the last step onto the sandy ground of the shore. Just beneath the cliff was a glittering grotto and an aquamarine pond. Leaning down to touch the water, she found it was cool. One could look straight down to the smooth, sandy bottom below. Jasmine glanced about at the dark horizon.

"What do you think?" he asked her.

"The way it's tucked under the cliff, it's almost as if we are the only two people left on earth."

They sat next to one another on one of the polished granite stones spread across the shore beneath the cliff. The clouds above them cleared to reveal a bright star-filled sky. Here, tucked away from all the world, with Ali by her side, they seemed to glitter particularly vividly.

"It's the strangest thing to be here with you. I'd just

about written you off when I saw you dancing at the Harvest Festival." She turned to him. "I didn't think you'd have room in your life for anyone but yourself."

"I will never live that down, will I?" he laughed.

"Nope." Jasmine shook her head and rested her head against his shoulder. "You're going to have to deal with that one forever."

Ali smiled.

Forever. Jasmine blinked. Had she just said that so easily? And yet, in this moment, she wished so much for that to be true. With the stars twinkling above and the waves gently hitting the shore, this was exactly what she wanted. To know this man who sat beside her forever. He was so easy to talk to, but sitting in silence next to him was just as comfortable.

This was the perfect way to end the most perfect night, but glancing at Ali now, she saw he looked preoccupied.

"What's the matter?" she asked.

"Oh, it's nothing, really. Sometimes my mind can wander. Can't shut it off no matter how hard I try."

"What are you thinking about right now?"

"I guess it's just being in Ababwa. I mean *back*. It makes me realize I'm not the person I want to be."

"Oh, Ali." She looked up at him. "You have to forgive yourself for what happened with that man at the restaurant."

"It's not that. I mean, it's more than just him." He looked at Jasmine and hesitated. "I want to be a certain kind of person. Sometimes I'm afraid no matter how hard I try, I'll never be the person I could be."

"I feel that way sometimes, too," she said. "Since I can't be the leader I want to be."

"No." He shook his head. "You're different. You *are* a leader."

"Oh, yes," she laughed bitterly. "Telling Dalia when it's time to draw my bath? Figuring out what my evening meal might be? I'm quite the leader all right."

"Even if you're not ruling Agrabah like you deserve to, you're still a leader through and through. Jasmine"—he turned to look at her, his eyes squarely on hers—"you are the smartest person I have ever met. You're kind and warm and generous. Even if you aren't an actual leader of Agrabah yet, you are a leader at heart."

"Ali . . ." Jasmine felt her eyes growing wet. "Thank you. I can't begin to tell you how much this time in your kingdom has meant to me. The way you let me sit with you on your advisory meeting, and helping Zaria and Maha . . . It felt good to be needed."

"No matter where you are, you will always be needed."

"Thank you," Jasmine said. And then, she realized something. "And I think the country I am needed in most is Agrabah," she said slowly. "I love it here in Ababwa. I truly do. It's the most charming kingdom I've ever been in. I know you were only joking back there at the menagerie about staying here forever and never going back, but there was a part of me that thought, 'Why *not* just stay here?' My opinion actually matters here. I can make a difference. In just one short day, I *have* made a difference. Your subjects, most of them, are so kind and helpful. As far as a kingdom goes this one is as good as it gets, but . . ."

"You want to go back."

"Being here I realize even more how much I am truly needed at home. Maybe I will never be as great and beloved by my people as you are here, but it's a goal worth trying for. And even if my father and Jafar don't think I can or should rule, I need to fight for the chance for my people. I need a seat at the table so I can help decide matters that affect the kingdom. Ruling for the sake of power only helps the powerful. Agrabah needs people in charge who care for both the kingdom and the people who live there. They deserve it."

"Not only does Agrabah need a good leader," Ali said, "Agrabah needs *you*. After spending this day with you, I know this much at least. Even if nothing else is real in this world, you are."

Waves crashed in the distance as they gazed at one another. There it was again. The way he looked at her could still every worry within her. It could make her forget everything. And right now, the way the moonlight reflected against his face, something about his eyes was so warm and so familiar. . . . There was no way to explain it: she knew him. It was as though she always had. He leaned closer to her. *He's going to kiss me*, she realized with a flutter in her chest. She closed her eyes and leaned closer. And then . . .

"Prince Ali!"

In an instant Ali and Jasmine pulled apart. Omar hurried down the stairs toward them.

"Omar!" Ali jumped up from the boulder and rushed toward him. The butler's forehead was coated with sweat.

"I'm so glad I found you. I was looking everywhere. I

didn't know what to do. I'm afraid we have a problem," he managed to say. "I don't know how it happened. It's never happened before. No one would ever dare . . ."

"What's wrong?" Ali asked.

"Are you all right?" asked Jasmine.

"The magic carpet." Omar breathed in ragged gasps. "It's missing."

Aladdin

Chapter Fourteen

ALADDIN AND JASMINE rushed up the stony cliff steps, through the meadow, and down the walkway toward the palace. They didn't stop until they were at last back in the living room with the gray sofas and the portraits of his parents.

"It was here." Aladdin panted and pointed to the ground. "I told it to rest right there before we left." And yet Omar was right. The space where the magic carpet had lain down earlier was now empty; marble tiles gleamed where it should have been.

"Carpet?" Aladdin called out. "If you're joking, now is a good time to come on out!"

He glanced around the palace, but nothing happened. The magic carpet did not appear. And while it was true that the carpet had a mischievous streak a mile wide, it had never played hide-and-seek in this way before.

Aladdin searched behind the sofas; he peeked behind the bookshelves. Jasmine hurried to check under the dining table and walked through the kitchen calling out for it.

"I didn't see it," Jasmine said once she returned to Aladdin.

"Me either." Aladdin felt dizzy. "I don't understand."

"Perhaps it went exploring in the bedrooms? It's easy to get lost in a place as large as this."

"There's also the palace grounds." Aladdin nodded.

"And the carpet loves animals, right? It's possible it just went over to the menagerie for some company."

"Maybe," Aladdin said hopefully.

"I'll ask the stable hand to explore the menagerie at once." Omar hurried out of the living room.

"It makes no sense," Aladdin said. "I know the carpet loves exploring, but it's never disobeyed me like this before." Just then, he noticed the tailor standing off to the side. She seemed to be a serious sort of woman to begin with, but right now her face looked positively ashen.

Their eyes met.

"I'm so sorry, Prince Ali," she said, her lower lip trembling. "I'm afraid that the carpet is not off in the menagerie or upstairs in any of the rooms."

"You saw what happened?" Aladdin rushed toward her. "Who was it? Did someone come and take it?"

"I didn't see anyone take it, per se, but a little while ago someone arrived at the palace. You remember him, Your Majesty? The one who came to the advisory meeting who you had asked me to measure and stitch new clothing for?"

Aladdin's stomach sank.

"He came earlier than I'd expected, so the servants escorted him here to wait for me. I had told him I would be right back after I retrieved the clothing for him to try on. Just to see if they fit all right. When I brought back the outfit, the man was gone. I didn't think much of it at the time, but when we discovered that the magic carpet had gone missing . . ."

"It must have been him," Jasmine said. "I remember how he stared at the carpet when he came to speak to us. He couldn't take his eyes off it."

"I didn't see him take it," the tailor said carefully. "It's possible the carpet did indeed slip out or get up to something, but I must admit that man made me uncomfortable. I am so sorry, Prince Ali. I shouldn't have left him alone. It's just that theft in the palace has never been an issue before."

"This isn't your fault," Aladdin assured her. His thoughts drifted back to the council meeting. That man had appeared a bit strange. The way he'd fixated on the gold-framed paintings and examined everything with an exacting stare. Aladdin had waved it all away at the time because the man's life didn't seem like it had been an easy one. And people who grew up struggling could understandably be a bit rough around the edges. But it was more than that, Aladdin now realized. Unlike the others who had come to the open forum and requested the prince's assistance with things, this man hadn't even *asked* for the new clothes the tailor fitted him for. That had been all Aladdin's idea. The man wasn't there to ask for help or advice. He was there to case the place. And when he'd seen the magic carpet flutter awake for that brief moment, the man must have realized exactly what he wanted.

Aladdin kicked himself. How could he have let down his guard? He had grown careless, and now the carpet was gone. He wondered what that man was doing to the magic carpet right now. Where could he have taken it? What could an imaginary man possibly want with a magic carpet?

Wondering did no good, though. Right now, finding the carpet was critical.

Suddenly, Aladdin realized what he needed to do.

"I'll be right back," he told Jasmine. "I have to do something upstairs—look through a few things that might help us figure out where the carpet could have gone."

"While you do that, I'll talk to the servants to see if we can't piece together exactly what happened. And there's still the chance it slipped out through an open door. It's best not to rule anything out."

"Thank you, Jasmine. I don't know what I'd do without you."

"Don't worry," she reassured him. "Wherever it went off to, we'll find it."

Aladdin raced up one of the golden staircases to the second story. He rushed past golden vases lit by special lights to showcase their fine artistic details and floor-to-ceiling paintings of flowers and trees. Ordinarily he would have paused to take this all in. But there was no time to linger tonight.

Aladdin yanked open the first door he came across and locked it firmly behind him. Looking around, he realized it was the palace library with walls covered in shelves that held more books than he'd seen in a lifetime. Stuffed ottomans lined the back windows. Jasmine would have loved it.

Aladdin paced the plush oversized rug in the center of the room and pulled the lamp out of his satchel in case it would help Genie hear him better from all the way in this imaginary kingdom. Guilt coursed through him. If only he'd been as concerned about keeping the carpet safe as he had been about the lamp. He cleared his throat.

"Genie," Aladdin said in a low voice. "I'm in a bit of trouble. I hope you can hear me, because I really need you right now."

"At your service." Just like that, Genie was there.

"Wow. That was fast!" Aladdin said.

"When the boss beckons, I appear. You know all you gotta do is ask!"

Aladdin breathed a sigh of relief. Just the sight of his blue friend made him feel better. Genie had created this kingdom, so Genie would have to address the technical difficulties that cropped up. Fixing glitches had to be part of the deal.

"You really do have a knack for the worst timing, though." Genie frowned at Aladdin. "I mean, I know the whole point of me distracting Princess Jasmine's hand-maiden was to be your wingman, but *boy*, is she charming and funny and beautiful. Do you have any idea the lin-guistic gymnastics I had to play to get away gracefully? Do you know what I told her?" He smacked his head with his hand. "I said I thought the camel float was hav-ing some issues. The camel float. I'm a magical genie, but clearly even my powers have their limits on smooth talk-ing! Anyhow, how's it going here?" He glanced around the empty library quarters. "Can't be going too great if you've locked yourself up in this library—which is very nicely decorated, if I don't say so myself."

"Not going good at all. I ran into a bit of trouble—" Aladdin began, but Genie interrupted.

"I must admit I'm a little disappointed." He shook his head. "You had a whole 'Genie day' to wow her. I'm afraid it may be a little late for any advice, sorry to say."

"That's not why I called you," Aladdin said impatiently. "Jasmine and I were getting along great. Perfectly, in fact. It was a dream come true. I think . . . no, I know . . . I *love* her, Genie. I really do."

"That's fantastic, kid!" Genie smiled. "So, what's the problem?"

"The magic carpet. It's missing."

"What do you mean it's missing?"

"It's disappeared."

"You didn't tell it to stay put?"

"I told it to rest while we went out into town. But if it didn't run away, it's—"

"No way did it run away," Genie interrupted. "It's not possible for a magic carpet to just up and flee. They're not built that way. It can be full of shenanigans, to be sure, but following directions it does very well."

"I think it was stolen. By someone here in the kingdom. The kingdom you invented."

"You're saying one of my inventions stole the carpet?"

Genie 's eyes widened. "That's impossible. Goes against the whole architecture of the town."

"Well, there must have been some sort of glitch. It's not your fault. Mistakes happen," Aladdin reassured him. "I was hoping to call you out here to see what went wrong and fix it."

"Well, that's a first." Genie frowned. "Which one do you think took it?"

"It was a man. He had a wiry build. Silvery hair. Gray eyes. He smelled like salt water, and his clothes were tattered, but they were green."

"Wiry build. Salt water. Silver hair." Genie's frown deepened. "Don't remember anyone like that. I based my people on those one of us knows personally. And the tattered clothes don't fit my design aesthetic. You saw the little boy I modeled after you, didn't you? I put some patches on his elbows and knees to make it believable, but even he was pretty well-dressed given his circumstances. This guy can't be one of my creations. Doesn't fit the bill for it."

"Are you saying he's *real*, then?" Aladdin stared at Genie.

"That's the only explanation."

"But how? You said this place was deserted."

"I said *virtually* deserted," Genie corrected him. "This place has been famously deserted ever since a big earthquake about a decade or so ago. It is possible I missed one person. There's a lot of caves and craggy spots here. It happens."

"Well, what does he want with the rug when there was a palace of gold and riches for the taking?" Aladdin asked, perplexed.

"Beats me, kid." Genie shook his head. "Maybe he just wanted to take a joyride? Put it in his place for some home décor? Hard to know what was going through his head. I can tell you the motivations of anyone I made, but not him."

"We can't leave Ababwa without the magic carpet, though."

"No, you can't." Genie nodded. "It's the only way in and it's the only way out."

"You can take care of this, can't you? I mean, we were already pushing it with how long we've been here. You can help us get the magic carpet, can't you?"

"Of course. But don't worry—even though you've had

an entire day here, back in Agrabah they're still cleaning up from the harvest festival."

"That's great," Aladdin sighed, relieved. "So you can get back the magic carpet for us and then we can head on back and no one will be the wiser?"

"Absolutely. In a flash. Not a problem at all," Genie replied.

"Thank you so much, Genie." Aladdin smiled. How had he lived his life before his friend? He had the solution to everything.

He waited for Genie to swipe his hands in the air and bring back the magic carpet, but Genie simply stood there with his arms crossed. Waiting.

"Ahem." Genie cleared his throat, gesturing toward the lamp in Aladdin's hand. "I'm ready when you are, kid."

"What do you mean?" asked Aladdin. "I told you to please go ahead and find it. We don't have time to lose."

"I'll do it as soon as I can snap my fingers. All you have to do is say the magic words."

"Magic words? You mean I have to wish for the carpet to come back?"

"That's right."

"But . . ." Aladdin's mind raced. "Isn't this part of the

original wish? To get us back from Ababwa to Agrabah is kind of implied in the wish to come here in the first place, isn't it?"

"Nice try," Genie said. "I wish it worked that way but it doesn't. You got me on the loophole with making you a kingdom gratis, but there's no loophole for this. This person is operating outside of the kingdom I created. If he was an imaginary rogue character, I could have fixed it no problem under the manufacturer's warranty, but he's not one of mine. I wish there was a way around it, but rules are rules, and genies are nothing if not bound by rules they wish they didn't have to follow. I'm really sorry, kid."

"No. That can't be," Aladdin said frantically. "There's got to be some wiggle room."

"Afraid you're all out of wiggle room. Just say the words and it's all fixed. Otherwise, I can't help you. And not to tell you what to do with your wishes or anything but when it comes to strategic wish making, this seems like a good one to make. You have to leave the kingdom of Ababwa eventually."

"But I can't use up a wish. Not on this. Not yet."

"What are you going to do, then?"

"I don't know. I'll try to figure it out and find the carpet on my own."

"You sure?"

"Yeah," Aladdin said reluctantly. "I'm sure."

"I can understand that." Genie nodded. "You know how to find me if you need me. Stay safe, little friend. And good luck."

Aladdin watched Genie disappear. He stared at the empty space where his friend had stood just seconds earlier. A chill ran through him as he thought about the man who'd stolen the carpet. It was one thing to have thought the thief was someone from Genie's imagination. But it was an entirely different feeling to realize that this was a *real* person.

And though this man had fooled Aladdin once, he would not fool him again.

Aladdin vowed to find the magic carpet if it was the last thing he ever did.

Jasmine

Chapter Fifteen

ASMINE'S HANDS were propped on her hips when Ali joined her in the living room.

"Any luck?" he asked her.

"I wish. Didn't find it anywhere. What about you? Did you find what you were looking for?"

"Nothing that could help us, unfortunately."

"Well, I'm glad you're back." She gestured to the team of worried-looking servants and guards who stood in a group. "I didn't want to waste time while you were upstairs, so I went ahead and assembled the servants and guards to figure out how we can best look for the carpet. The more people searching, the better."

"Princess Jasmine thought perhaps I and the other kitchen staff could head into town to inform the people of what happened," the chef said.

"The guards and I can go door-to-door to see if the man lives in any of the homes in town," said the head guard.

"We'll go to the meadows and check the shores by the cliffside," a gardener said.

"I think between all of us dividing and searching certain areas, we'll be the most effective," Jasmine said. "What do you think?" She hesitated as she took in Ali's worried expression. She hoped he didn't think she was presumptuous for taking charge of his palace in this way.

"This is brilliant," Ali said. "Thank you, Jasmine."

Everyone hurried off to search for the carpet. The palace walls echoed with worried conversation.

"I'm glad everyone is helping," Ali said. "But I can't stay here just waiting. I have to do something."

"Who said anything about waiting?" Jasmine raised

an eyebrow. "Seeing you personally searching will under-score the gravity of what is going on. Besides, people may open up to you in ways they won't to anyone else."

"You've thought of everything," Ali said.

"I know you love that carpet." Jasmine squeezed Ali's arm. "I have grown pretty fond of it myself. We'll find it. We will make sure we do."

Together they hurried down the front steps, out the palace gates, and toward the village square. Rounding the corner, they ran into a man—the same one who had confronted the young boy, Jamaal, earlier at the town square. His eyes widened when he saw them.

"Just saw the palace guards rush past me on my way home for the night," he said. "Is there trouble?"

"Someone stole something valuable from the palace," Ali told him. "Have you seen him, by any chance? He had gray eyes and silvery hair. He'd have had a rolled-up carpet with him. It is very valuable to us and we must find it as soon as possible."

The man frowned and then shook his head emphatically. "No, Prince Ali. I can't remember seeing anyone who fits that description . . . and I'd certainly have noticed someone running about with a rolled-up carpet tucked under their arm. Of that I am sure. But I'll be on the lookout for him now." The man's jaw tightened. "Stealing from the prince of Ababwa? The sheer nerve! That is downright treason. Don't you worry, Prince Ali, we will find him and bring him to justice as soon as possible. I will begin searching at once."

Jasmine and Ali thanked the man and continued on their way. By the time they'd reached the town square, news of the theft had spread throughout the kingdom. People rushed to and fro, speaking in hushed tones. Torchlights and lanterns lit the path as people scoured the area for any sign of the man who had stolen the magic carpet.

"Do you think he flew away with it?" Jasmine asked Ali.

"I can't imagine the carpet would let him do that," Ali said. "At least I don't think so."

"Such a sweet rug. It must be so terrified right now. I hope wherever it is, it's not being hurt."

"Me too."

Jasmine looked about at the worried expressions of the townspeople they passed along the way. Beyond the square, she saw the hilly peaks and the docks in the distance. Boats rocked gently in the breeze from where they were anchored at the port.

"Everything appears to be in order. Same number of vessels as when we flew in," Ali said as he followed her gaze and squinted at the boats. "But I'll have a guard make sure nothing is amiss there."

If the carpet was injured or in any way unable to take them back to Agrabah by air, Jasmine wondered how long it would take to get back home on one of those ships. What state of mind would her father be in when he discovered her missing from her palace suite? Ali had explained to her that time moved differently when traveling by a magical carpet, but surely they were pushing it now. Sooner or later someone would figure out she was missing.

But there was no sense in worrying about any of that right now. They simply needed to find the magic carpet. Whether they left by carpet or by boat, the only way she would ever go back was together with their friend, the carpet.

Aladdin

Chapter Sixteen

*H*OW COULD *I have been so careless?*
Aladdin fumed as they hurried down the streets of Ababwa. The streets were lit by the moon above and the glow of lanterns held by townspeople hurrying past, searching for the magic carpet. He knew it did no good to blame himself, but he'd messed up the one thing he had to do—the most important thing—taking care of the magic carpet. It was their only way into the kingdom and their only way out. He could have asked a guard to

keep an eye on it. How hard would that have been? How could he not have done such a simple thing?

He thought back to the crook. Aladdin had projected himself onto the man, hadn't he? He knew what it was to be poor, what it was to not have proper clothing and to feel frustrated and hungry. But he had compared and sympathized so much he'd failed to see the man for the individual he was, with his own motivations and ambitions. Aladdin had completely and utterly missed what was happening. Now that he looked back on their first meeting, the man *had* stared at the carpet a beat too long. It should have been obvious then and there that something was amiss. With a new title, fresh surroundings, and adoring subjects, Aladdin had grown soft, and thanks to him the magic carpet had been stolen. What had that rug done to anyone to deserve this? It was just a sweet, lovable being that had never harmed anyone and had brought them all this way. He cringed at his last memories with the magic carpet. It had wanted so badly to accompany them and explore the streets of Ababwa together. They'd told it to stay back. They had said no.

Aladdin hoped the magic carpet could hang on long enough for them to find it.

"A rug shop!" Jasmine pointed to a store they were walking past. They paused and took in the glass window with a display of multicolored rugs.

"Well, it's worth looking at," Aladdin said. He was pressing a hand to the door handle when three guards turned the corner and approached them.

"Any luck?" Aladdin asked, turning to them.

"Unfortunately, no." The tallest guard shook his head. "I wish we had some information—any information—to share. But so far no one has seen a hint of this man at all. We were just coming to our final place to check, this rug shop, before we came back to the palace to update you."

"Thank you for trying," Aladdin said.

"Everyone in the kingdom is searching. Zaid, the lantern shop owner—he lent out all his lanterns to everyone. People are scouring every bit of forest, the lagoons, the dock, and the pier as well. We'll keep looking until we find it. After we check the rug shop, we will double back to make certain we didn't miss anything."

"Why don't you go ahead and double back now?

Jasmine and I can check out the rug shop. Thank you again for your help with all of this."

"Yes, sir." The guard saluted Aladdin, and the trio turned and hurried back toward the town square.

Aladdin watched them leave and then looked doubtfully at the shop in front of them.

"It's possible," Jasmine said. "Perhaps the magic carpet wanted to meet some of its compatriots, or maybe the man has the carpet stowed away here to throw us off his trail. What better way to hide than in plain sight?"

Stepping inside the shop, Jasmine and Aladdin were confronted by a dizzying array of rugs of all shapes, colors, and sizes. Some hung from hooks in the ceiling, others lay ten to a pile across the shop floor, and more were rolled up in cubbies on the far wall. Aladdin walked over to one hanging carpet. It had the same colors and pattern as his friend, but Aladdin didn't need to touch it to know it was not his magic carpet. You couldn't taste or touch or smell the magic that the carpet exuded, but you knew when you were around it that you were in the presence of something beyond what anyone had ever seen. The carpets in this shop were lovely, but they were not magical. None of them was his friend.

"What is that man doing with the carpet?" Aladdin shook his head. "What if he's hurting it? What if the carpet won't even be able to fly at all once we get to it?"

"Well, as long as we can find it, we can always leave some other way."

"How?"

"By boat."

"Oh," Aladdin mumbled. "Well . . ."

"I know. A boat is not the way I would want to go back to Agrabah, either. It will certainly take longer, and there's no way around the fact that it will come out that I went missing. But let's not worry about worst-case scenarios just yet. Let's focus on finding the carpet. We have other ways if we need them."

Aladdin said nothing. He couldn't tell her the truth. What would he say? That the boats she found comfort in couldn't take them anywhere beyond the horizon of Ababwa? What would become of them upon a boat like that?

"I still can't figure out where that man disappeared to," Jasmine said. "He must live outside the kingdom. It's the only reasonable explanation."

"There is some undeveloped land," Aladdin said slowly.

He remembered seeing it when they had first flown into the kingdom. "It's past the docks toward the rockier cliffs that border the kingdom. He could be there."

"He did smell as though he lived directly by the ocean," Jasmine said. "He must have grabbed the magic carpet and headed out to the less populated parts of Ababwa, where he knew people wouldn't think to check."

Aladdin remembered the coastline he'd seen when they had flown over. "But it's miles long," he said. "Where would we even begin?" He had to find the thief on his own without Genie's help—he *had* to. And yet, he thought of the jagged cliff-laden shoreline and wondered how he could possibly do it alone; they had deployed the entire town to help them find the magic carpet and were no closer than when they began their search.

"The cartography shop!" Jasmine exclaimed. "It's right there." She pointed across the street. The light was still on inside. "That's where we should have started from the very beginning. Let's check the local maps. That way we can at least get the lay of the land out there, what sort of places someone might hide away. It could help us narrow down the places that this man might be."

Aladdin hoped Jasmine was right and that Ahmed

had some sort of map in his shop that could help them. It was worth a try. Anything was worth it if it could lead them to the carpet. If this didn't work, Aladdin knew he would be out of options. He'd have to call for Genie and use the lamp.

From *LEGENDARY LEADERS ACROSS THE AGES—*
"Musa Saleem, or: The Man Who Spoke to Bulls"

SALEEM HAD been keeping a secret for a long time. It was a secret he'd kept so long he sometimes wondered if it was merely a story he'd told himself. And yet, he thought of his mother—her silvery blue eyes and her hands worn from laboring in the fields, tending to their vegetable gardens, and milking the goats—and his father, small in stature and rough in demeanor, who said such qualities were simply how one survived in what they did for a living. And Saleem would remember again how real his past was. It wasn't his family he wished to hide; he loved his family. What they did for a living was the true source of Saleem's shame.

His family spoke to bulls. Some would hear this and take it metaphorically, thinking what one meant was simply that they were so well equipped at their work of raising, training, and caring for bulls that it was as though they could speak to them. But in fact, his family had a gift of speaking in the particular animal language of the bull. His family could calm their rage. Convince them to give the neighboring farm's cow a calf. Because they understood their language, they respected these giant creatures, and though the family could have made far more money if they'd trained and sold bulls for bullfighting, as was the custom of most bull breeders, the family knew a life in a bullring was not what any bull desired. The money would have been nice, his father often said, but he couldn't live with the knowledge that they'd played a hand in the inevitable fate of a bull's grisly death. So they lived on their acre of land and helped neighboring farms with breeding, calming, and selling bulls to distant pastures. Though it never amounted to much, a simple existence was all the family had ever known. They got by somehow, and they were content enough with their circumstances.

Except Musa Saleem.

Of course, back then, he had not been Musa Saleem. He was Musa Bullknower, the surname as undignified a name as one could have. He loathed the manure and the stench that never left his skin even after scrubbing under scalding water in the tub. He hated the heat of the oppressive outdoors and the sheer difficulties of their circumstances. His parents were grateful for their plot of land, handed down from generation to generation, but the square patch owned *him* more than the other way around—a lifetime prison sentence he could not commute. When he read the books the kind local bookshop owner lent him from time to time, Musa dreamed of the characters in those tales and longed for a life beyond the one that was his destiny.

And then one day, he stopped dreaming and began planning.

Step one was to look the part he wanted to play. After years of saving and secreting away money, Musa had enough to pay the local tailor to make him a splendid outfit. "An outfit fit for a king," the tailor declared after he'd finished. Indeed, the navy outfit that Musa ran his hand over was the finest material he'd ever touched in his life.

The next step was to purchase a book—his first one—from the surprised bookshop owner. The book was entitled *Manners and Mannerisms of Proper Society*. He read the book cover to cover in secret until he had memorized all its contents, and then he burned it.

The final step was the most difficult: his departure. There was nothing for him in these farmlands. He had to travel to the heart of the kingdom, where the rural landscape melted away into the city proper. What would happen then, Musa didn't know, but staying where he was wasn't an option. And so, the next evening, as his parents looked on with tears in their eyes, Musa waved goodbye and stepped onto the dirt road that eventually led to town.

A handful of coins secured him a ride with a passing caravan, and by dawn he arrived. Musa marveled at the city sights. Shops stacked upon shops, and streets full of people and carriages.

Before Musa could wonder what exactly he would do

now, a golden pumpkin-shaped carriage passed by, and a pebble from a horse trotting past dislodged from the ground and flew into its spoke. The carriage halted with a sudden jerk.

Musa hurried over and poked the pebble off the spoke. It slid effortlessly to the ground.

"Thank you, good man." A prince popped his head out of the window.

Musa flinched. He hated how people's expressions crumpled upon looking at him closer, their noses scrunching up at the smell he could not hide. But this prince smiled at him. Then Musa remembered his fine navy clothes; he looked nothing like the bull keeper he was.

"I'm Prince Kashif. What's your name?" the prince asked.

"I am . . . Saleem." Musa thought quickly. "I am here from Sulamandra," he improvised, using the name of a nearby kingdom he'd heard much about recently.

"Ah, that fire." The prince nodded sympathetically. "It was as bad as they say it was?"

"Oh, yes." Musa nodded emphatically. "It was very tragic. It's why I'm here."

"What sort of work did you do?"

"What did I do? Well, I did many things. Um, I advised, mostly," he said. "Or rather, listened. I'm a good listener for people who need to untangle their thoughts—sometimes a listening ear can be the greatest solution to the most difficult problems."

A listener? Musa cringed. What sort of profession was this to have made up?

"Never heard of a professional listener," the prince said. "But I like the sound of it. I'm on my way home and I could use a good set of ears for a situation I'm dealing with. I'll pay you for your time. Let's see how it goes?"

Musa's heart surged with joy, and he climbed aboard the carriage.

One day turned to two, and then three, and soon Prince Kashif found Musa's presence indispensable. Musa's listening ears were truly the trick the prince needed to untangle his thoughts.

As the years passed and Musa's status grew, he thought of his parents often. He sent them money regularly, but he knew it wasn't money they longed for—they wanted their son. But he was not their son anymore. He was Saleem now—confidant to the prince, from a land across the sea. And though he liked the idea of this new identity, the true person within felt like a sagging weight.

One day, Kashif approached Saleem for a private word.

"You have been immeasurably helpful to me," he told Saleem. "My father and I agree that it's time I had my own advisor. And though you are an official listener, I would like to offer that position to you. It is a role of great trust, and I trust no one else more than you."

Saleem swallowed. It was an honor; one he couldn't have imagined when he'd arrived to this kingdom proper with hardly anything but a few coins all those years ago. But he felt a pang of guilt—Prince Kashif placed his trust in him, and Saleem hadn't been honest about who he was.

Seeing the hesitation upon Saleem's face, the prince smiled.

"Of course, you don't have to decide right this moment. Think about it," the prince reassured him. "In the meantime, come along with me to a great sporting match. I'm ashamed I haven't taken you to one yet. You will love it."

Before Saleem could ask what sort of sport it was,

they were off in the carriage. People lined the streets and shouted in excitement. As they neared, Saleem's heart dropped. The large stadium. The endless rows of seats.

"A bullfight," Saleem said weakly.

"Yes," the prince said. "Had you ever heard of this sport back in Sulamandra?"

Saleem swallowed as they took their seats.

A man in a tight black uniform entered the ring. He flashed his feathers with a flourish.

"Ladies and gentlemen!" an announcer bellowed. "Welcome to the two hundred fiftieth annual competition! Tonight, we have a special honor. Prince Kashif has graced us with his presence."

The crowd rejoiced and chanted for the prince. He waved a hand and smiled.

"Will you bless us with a few kind words before we begin?" the man implored the prince.

Everyone cheered, and so the prince took the steps leading to the ring.

"Thank you." The prince turned to the crowd. He spoke of his joy of leading the kingdom and extended his well-wishes to the bullfighter for the match to come. As he spoke, Saleem startled. The bull that was to be locked in its cage was free. The gate had come undone. It slowly made its way toward the people standing in the center of the ring.

Before Saleem could cry out a word of warning, the bull charged the ringmaster, who crumpled to the ground. The crowd grew deathly silent as the prince turned, his face pale as the bull now leaned and kicked at the ground. The bull's handlers were running toward it and shouting at it to stop at once, but the animal's eyes were bloodred with anger.

The prince would be next. In an instant, Saleem raced down the steps into the ring, running straight to the bull.

"No, Saleem!" shouted the prince. "Don't!"

But Saleem was not Saleem now. He was Musa Bullknower. He walked up to the bull and asked it to lay down its guard. He understood the bull's hunger. The pain the trainers had inflicted. He urged the bull to exercise calm. He hadn't spoken to an animal in so long, and yet those dormant parts of him came to life as strong as ever. At the sound of Musa's voice, the bull relaxed—and kneeled to the ground, like an obedient puppy.

As people whisked away the injured ringmaster and secured the bull back in its pen, the prince stared at his friend.

"You are a man of many talents, Saleem."

"I am not Saleem," he said quietly. "My name is Musa. Or at least, it once was. My family is from the farmlands and I spent my life here in this very kingdom raising and speaking to bulls. I lied to you when we first met. I was too ashamed of who I was. I do not deserve quarters in your palace or to be your trusted advisor. I am not the refined man you trusted."

He bit his lip, waiting for the prince to declare the measure of his disappointment.

"I do not judge you for where you came from," the prince said. "I judge you for the man you are. And you are refined and well-read and well-mannered, and you are also the son of bull speakers. And you saved my life today. You are both people, Saleem and Musa, and you have in my estimation risen tenfold for making your own mark in the world without any privilege to give you support or shade along the way. If you would be so willing as to take a seat as my advisor, I would name you Advisor Musa, or Advisor Saleem—whatever you would like to be called.

And I would be honored for you to help me lead. Do you accept my position?"

"Perhaps we can find a way to modify this sport so it may entertain the people but not hurt the animals in this manner?"

"Sound counsel." Prince Kashif nodded. "We shall. Does this mean you accept?"

Musa Saleem smiled then. He said yes.

Jasmine

Chapter Seventeen

*A*HMED WAS poring over a gray map spread out on an angled table when Jasmine and Ali stepped into his shop. The front door chimed as they closed the door. When he looked up and saw them, his eyes widened.

"Prince Ali. Princess Jasmine. I heard about what happened. The theft. I'm so sorry. I hope they find whoever did it as soon as possible. I was looking at a map of Ababwa right here to see if there were any passages or tunnels we haven't explored yet. Haven't turned up anything yet, but I'm going to keep on looking."

"Thank you so much for that," Jasmine said. "We were here because we were wondering if we could take a look at any local maps you might have that detail the undeveloped portions of Ababwa?"

"You think he's out there?" The man stood up and scratched his chin. "Desolate and hard to really survive on the cliffside. I don't believe there are any dwellings out in that part of the region. Those rocks are slippery, and the salty sea spray from the cliffs makes it an unpleasant place to be for long."

"Perhaps he's choosing to hide there because all those things will make it all the trickier for us to find him."

"Well, that does make sense." He nodded. "I have one map that might be able to help you. It's still a work in progress, as I'm making it myself." He removed a key from his drawer, walked over to a tall bookshelf, and unlocked a cabinet. Pulling out a scroll, he spread it across the table.

"This one shows the broad strokes of the undeveloped region of Ababwa. I began labeling the cliffs and valleys, just as a little fun hobby for myself. It's not an official map per se, and it's been ages since I looked at the thing."

Jasmine pressed her hands against the map and traced the edge of the land that jutted above the shore. "Ababwa is much larger than I realized," she said slowly. She gestured toward the miles and miles of sandy cliffs and shorelines.

"There are so many hideaway spots." Ali shook his head. "Look at all these caves and coves. He could be anywhere."

"And the land is treacherous," Ahmed warned. "Been there myself a few times to map it all out and more often than not walked away with scratches and bruises. Unless you know where on the map he actually went, it will be like trying to find one particular pearl in a great wide ocean."

"I know where he went!" a small voice shouted.

"Where did that sound come from?" Jasmine said with a startle.

"Up here. You're right under my nose."

Looking up, Jasmine saw him. Jamaal, the boy from the marketplace. He was perched on the old wooden rafters of the store, watching them with wide-eyed wonder.

A glass lantern swayed on a nearby rafter, showing the path he'd taken.

"How on earth did you get up there?" Jasmine asked.

"The bookshelf," both Jamaal and Ali said at once.

"Every day that boy winds up somewhere that makes no sense." Ahmed shook his head. "Will you get down from there before you break your neck and my rafters?"

"Sorry." The boy grinned sheepishly before shimmying from the rafters to a wall and climbing down an oak bookshelf filled with books of maps.

"Better landing this time," Ahmed said pointedly to the boy.

"You know where he went?" Jasmine asked the boy.

"Yes." Jamaal nodded. "I mean, I think so. I was sitting on the apothecary store's rooftop and saw a man in a tattered outfit hurrying away from town. I didn't think much of it, but after hearing what everyone around town was talking about and the descriptions of the man, I think it's got to be him. It was too dark to make out if he was holding anything, but he was heading over to the craggy cliffs past the docks and pier—to the left. The spot where all those caves crowd together. It must be him."

"Makes sense," Ahmed said. "He must be heading to

the 'Phoenix Trio.' I named it that because the three boulders that lean into a cradle of sorts look like feathers from afar. It's the rockiest part of the land—the waves crash louder there, and there are many caves one can hide in." He pointed to a detailed spot on the map. "Even though it's the closest spot to Ababwa proper, it's the trickiest to navigate because of all those caves. I suppose that's why he went there."

"Have you ever been out there?" Ali asked Jamaal.

"No." The boy shook his head. "I got close once, but it's a little scary."

"How far away is it?" Jasmine asked.

"It's probably no more than eight minutes flat if I run really fast." Jamaal hurried toward the door. "Just follow me. I can take you there."

"No!" Jasmine and Ali said at the same time. Just like that, the boy's eager expression faded.

"I can do it, though," he said quietly. "I know this town like the back of my hand."

"Oh, no, it's not that. I'm sure you could lead us straight to him," Jasmine reassured him. "But the thing is, whoever he is, he's dangerous. You're young, and as you said yourself, it's a tricky place."

"But I owe you both. For forgiving me. For sparing my life. I want to help."

"You telling us where he might be is help enough," Ali said. "We'd have spent hours looking around fruitlessly if you hadn't."

"May we borrow this map?" Jasmine asked the shop owner.

"Of course." He nodded. "And when I see them, I'll let the guards know where you both have headed."

They thanked him and stepped outside the shop. Ali glanced at the road toward the pier and the boats swaying gently with the breeze. He hesitated for a moment before turning toward Jasmine.

"How about I just check out what the situation is?" he asked. "Maybe you could stay back here in Ababwa proper and see if you can help Ahmed summon the guards?"

Jasmine stared at him. "You're not serious, are you?"

"You heard Ahmed. It's dangerous out there with the slippery landscape and the caves. And this man may mean us harm. I don't want Jamaal to get himself injured, but I don't want you to get hurt either."

"If you're going, I'm going, and that's that."

"Jasmine, what if you—"

"I'm the one who is good with maps." She gestured to the scroll in her hands. "We won't find this place without it."

"Looks like there is no changing your mind," he said.

"We're in this together," she answered firmly.

The port that had looked inviting and regal in the daylight now looked ominous. With each step, they left the town square of Ababwa behind them.

"This is it." Jasmine squinted at the map. "The path."

"I can't make it out at all." Ali bent down to take a closer peek.

The path was covered in moss and grass, but taking a step upon it, they both felt solid cobblestone beneath their feet, buried beneath years of neglect. If not for the moonlight they'd have missed it entirely.

"Looks like it curves a bit," Ali observed. Indeed, they could see that the thin patches of moss twisted and turned up a slope and then out of sight. From where Jasmine stood, she could hear the crashing waters against the cliffs. She thought of the sea-salted rocks and the unsteady boulders and hesitated. And then she thought of the magic carpet and how it must have been feeling right at that exact moment.

"Let's go." She nodded.

Together both Jasmine and Ali walked down the curved path. The wind picked up, pushing against them, as though warning them to stay back. And though neither of them knew for certain where this path would take them, or who might await them at the other side, both knew they had to keep going. There was no other option.

Aladdin

Chapter Eighteen

*W*ITH THE MOON obscured by clouds, Jasmine's and Aladdin's eyes adjusted to the darkness until they could make out the landscape as they hurried down the path. Grainy pebbles underneath the damp moss crunched beneath their feet.

Following the map, they headed toward the site Ahmed had called the Phoenix Trio. The farther they walked, the more the landscape changed. It was so different here, in the parts of the land that Genie's magic had not touched. Not just the obvious differences of walking so close to cliffs and ocean shores, but the color and texture of this part of Ababwa was starkly different. Gone was the brilliant sheen that hung over Genie's charming cobblestoned streets, red and purple lanterns lighting the paths, and colorful curtains billowing out of windows; here there was almost no color at all. From the sky and the clouds floating above to the grass snaking across the trail and the deteriorated mountainscapes they walked by . . . everything here was—

"Gray," Jasmine said, looking around. "Maybe it's just because it's night and there are no lights here. But everything looks a little more somber here, doesn't it?"

Gray was the perfect word, Aladdin thought. This part of Ababwa felt as though an artist had begun a charcoal sketch but lost interest and wandered away.

The path curved again, taking them toward the edge of the cliffs. Jasmine and Aladdin took care with their steps, gripping one another's arms over slippery stones. They paused and peeked inside each dark cave that gaped at them along the way, but they were all empty. Just then a strong gust of wind rushed over to them. It made their clothing rustle and their hair flow backward.

"Wow." Jasmine covered her nose with her hand. "Do you smell that?"

"Salty. Like seaweed."

"Like that man."

They glanced about the desolate landscape and the hundreds of caves dotted along their line of sight. Where to begin?

"Wait." Aladdin pointed to a formation in the distance, three enormous boulders pressed together in a semicircle of sorts. "Their tips are narrow and angled like feathers, sort of how Ahmed said. Maybe those are the Phoenix Trio?"

"That must be it." Jasmine studied her map and nodded. "Yes, that's the place."

The terrain underfoot grew wetter as they walked toward the boulders. Jasmine and Aladdin gripped one another's hands to keep from falling. Beads of perspiration dotted Aladdin's forehead. Caves yawned at them along the walkway, the wind tunneling through them as they passed by, howls piercing the night sky and sending chills down their spines. They paused to take in all the hideaway spots.

"What if he's in one of these caves? What if he's

watching us right now? There are too many of them. He could find us first, and then what?"

"Wait," Jasmine whispered. "Look."

Aladdin followed her gaze, and then he saw it, too. At first, he was convinced his eyes were playing tricks on him. But there it was. Smoke billowed out from behind the Phoenix Trio. And then a flicker of light. Orange. It glowed from between the spaces of the boulders.

Quietly, Jasmine and Aladdin made their way toward the source of the light. Closer now, they saw that the boulders overlooked the jagged cliffs. They inched past cactus sprouting along the cliffside. And then both of them saw the opening—the gap between the boulders. The light glowed brighter. Everything felt like it had grown silent and still.

"It might be a trap. The flame is so bright," Jasmine finally said to Aladdin. "It feels like he's luring us there."

"Why don't you go and call for the guards?" he whispered.

"And what are you going to do?"

"I'll go talk to him until you can get them over here."

"I'm not leaving you alone with that man," she whispered.

"Jasmine, it's dangerous. We don't both have to put ourselves at risk like this."

"Are you serious? Do you honestly think I'll let you go in there alone?"

"I know, I know. I just don't want you getting hurt. Whatever is on the other side, it's not good."

"Two heads are better than one." Jasmine squeezed Aladdin's hand. "Let's go and see what is going on. We're getting the carpet back. No matter what."

"Okay." Aladdin nodded. Together they slipped through the large sandy boulders and onto the cliffside. Aladdin blinked as he got his bearings. Waves crashed loudly against the shore below. The flame that beckoned them had vanished.

"What is this place?" Jasmine said slowly.

Jasmine had been right, Aladdin realized. This *had* been a trap. And they'd fallen right into it. He brushed his hands against his clothing—he'd been in such a rush to rescue his beloved magic carpet, he hadn't brought so much as a kitchen knife to defend himself.

Before they could do anything, however, they heard a voice.

Low and gravelly.

Familiar.

A light flickered back on.

"Well, look who it is," someone said. "I must say, it took you both long enough."

Jasmine

Chapter Nineteen

THERE HE WAS. The man she had seen when they'd first arrived in the kingdom of Ababwa. The same man who'd surveyed the palace at the council meeting as though he'd wished to devour everything whole. And while she'd known it would be him, seeing him in person and up close—his eyes gleaming, the sinister smile spreading across his face as he watched them from the edge of the cliff—made her insides go cold. His silvery hair flapped across his forehead.

The fire within the glass lantern which had faded

seconds earlier now roared back to life, glowing orange and angry in his hand. A knife under his arm glinted against the moonlight. And under his other arm, there it was. Jasmine's heart sank. Squeezed tightly and rolled up: the magic carpet. It wiggled and squirmed against the man's impossibly tight grip. She wanted to rush right up to it and yank it away from this horrible man's arms. But she dared not move a muscle, afraid of the harm he could do before she could so much as take a step.

"Carpet," Ali shouted out. "We're going to get you out of this! I promise."

At the sound of Ali's voice, the magic carpet squeezed and struggled harder, batting its entire body against the man's rib cage.

"That is enough of that now," the man snarled. He jabbed a knee directly into the carpet's middle. It crumpled on impact.

"Stop hurting it!" Jasmine shouted. She took a step toward the man, but he raised his lantern in warning.

"Come closer and see what else I can do. I've been playing nicely so far, but you don't want to know what I will do when I get angry," the man said. "Stay right where you are or you will regret it, you have my word."

"Unhand it, immediately," said Ali, who seemed to boil over with rage. He clenched his fists. "You let it go this instant and I can be lenient with your sentence."

"My sentence?" The man barked out a laugh. "I must say, I didn't take you for a comedian when I first saw you. You're not in any position to demand or threaten me with anything. Besides, who are you fooling?" The man glowered. "You are no prince."

Before Ali could respond, the man turned toward Jasmine. "You." He nodded at her. "I know you. Recognized you as soon as I saw you on that carriage ride, in fact. You look so much like your mother it took me a minute to be certain I was not hallucinating. Now *you* are true royalty. You are Princess Jasmine of the kingdom of Agrabah, aren't you?"

Jasmine stared at him. He knew who she was. And yet . . . who was *he*?

"A fine distance from your home, aren't you, Princess?" he asked. "Heard your daddy didn't like you going so far away alone. Did the locks break to your cage, or did you find the key? Or . . ."—he narrowed his eyes at Ali—"did this young man here kidnap you? In which case, perhaps this is a doubly rewarding day. Find a magic carpet, rescue a princess, and return her to her kingdom. For a handsome reward, no doubt."

"I don't need rescuing *or* returning," Jasmine snapped at him.

"Enough with the taunts." Ali placed his arm protectively around Jasmine. "Who are you and what is it that you want?"

Jasmine felt worry seeping out from Ali's body like an invisible cloud.

"Thought you'd never ask," the man said. "Name's Abbas. And I only want what anyone on this godforsaken land would want. To get the hell out of here."

He glanced at both Jasmine and Ali and shook his head.

"Look at the two of you. I see the way you look at me. The disgust. The condescension. I was once a great man, I'll have you know. Wealthy and full of privilege, the world in the palm of my hand."

"Were you a prince?" Jasmine asked cautiously. She looked at the carpet, still struggling against this man.

"I wasn't a prince." His expression darkened. "But what I should have been was a *sultan*. I could have been. I almost was. I was certainly smarter than Waleed."

"Sultan Waleed?" Jasmine's eyes widened. She knew of Sultan Waleed. Everyone did. He was one of the most generous sultans in the world, famous for his kindness and his mercy. And then, her eyes lit up. *Of course!* There was a story about him in her book of legendary leaders. She strained her memory to remember the story's specifics.

"*Sultan* Waleed," he scoffed. "What makes a man a king anyway? Just who his parents were and where he was born? That man was stupid and weak. I should know better than most; he called me his best friend, after all, and let down his guard around me. Literally *and* figuratively, which in and of itself underscores just how foolish he was. I'm one of the few people who knew him for what he really was. Ridiculous and utterly unworthy of the crown."

"So, you're the one . . ." She trailed off. She remembered the story now. How he had betrayed his best friend and the sultan of his country for the sake of greed. But this made no sense! What was that man from her book doing *here*?

"Ah," the man said as he saw the look of recognition

spread across Jasmine's face. "So you *have* heard of me, haven't you?"

"You're a legend."

"The wrong sort, I'm sure." The man frowned. "Alas. There is still time to undo the narrative and get my revenge. Your kingdom of Agrabah was one of the many I reached out to for support all those years ago, you know." His eyes narrowed. "And one of the many who did not reply to my calls for aid."

"We had no chance to reply before you burned the palace down," Jasmine improvised.

"Burned it down?" Abbas repeated. "They always make the man who didn't win the bad guy in the story-books, don't they? To the victor go the prizes and the chance to share their side of the story as the only true tale. That man had a whole powerful kingdom at his beck and call; cascading waterfalls and wealth unimaginable from all the minerals that lay buried within its soil. And that fool didn't know a thing to do with any of it. I was *trying* to do a favor for everyone by taking it over and ruling it like it needed to be ruled. Imagine how many people could have benefited if I had mined the gold and silver. And *he's* the good one? Hoarding it all and leaving it untouched just because he's too wealthy to need it? I was only thinking of the common man and what they needed. You all think he's wise and noble, but I know the real man." Abbas made a face as he mimicked him. " 'Oh, Abbas, how could you? Think of the trees and the animals. Abbas, I thought we were like brothers.' How could I *what*? Try to do what was best for the kingdom? He'll never admit to it, that sniveling toddler of a man, but he lunged for me first that night. It was only me and him in that room. Only my word against his, but I don't care what the history books say. I know the truth."

"That palace was beautiful," Jasmine murmured. She remembered reading about the architecture years ago. She'd seen the illustrations of its graceful arches and curves. The rose gardens of Sulamandra were world renowned.

"Yes, it was beautiful." Abbas sighed. And for the first time, she saw a look of genuine nostalgia and sadness spread across his face at the memory. "Now you tell me, why would I want to burn down the palace that was meant to be *mine*? The one I had practically grown up in alongside the sultan, and was on the brink of claiming for myself? I would have never done such a thing. But we do know who would've made such a foolish mistake, don't we? That's why he banished me here, you know. By putting me in no-man's-land, he hoped no one would learn the truth. But an earthquake saved the day and turned the prison into dust a short while ago. Now I must get out of here before the guards return and notice I'm not exactly imprisoned anymore. I will *not* be here when they come back. I won't stand for it!" Abbas's eyes glinted dangerously. He lowered his voice. "But I must give credit where credit is due. They did get one thing right in dumping me on this land. These waters are too treacherous to escape. Made some rafts once I broke free but can't get any farther than the rock outcroppings out over on the horizon before I'm pummeled back to this godforsaken place. But now"—he smiled down at the carpet, who still tried as hard it could to break free—"now I can finally leave."

"The carpet isn't going to take you anywhere." Ali glowered.

"That's true, it's a finicky little thing, isn't it?" Abbas glanced down at it. "I almost got it off the ground once, but the blasted thing flipped me right over almost immediately. And these boulders are harder than they look, especially when you fall from a bit of a height. Luckily, the hook and wire I stole from the supply shop in town kept it from running away. Scrappy fellow." He looked almost admiringly at it. "Got to give it that much. Even if it's going to end up doing exactly what I say sooner or later."

Jasmine saw the wire dangling on the ground; it snaked up against the carpet, and the metal shaped like a fishing hook sank deep within its body.

"You put a hook inside it?!" Ali cried. "How is it going to fly for you or anyone when you've maimed it?"

"Ah, so you suggest I take the hook out, do you? Nice try." Abbas smiled. "I take the hook out and this thing will head for the hills, so to speak."

"Keep the hook in and it will never fly for anyone again," Jasmine said. "It's a magical being, and it simply can't work that way."

"She's right," Ali said. "It won't fly for you. Or me. Or anyone else, for that matter."

"How about a compromise, then? People say those can be fun. I will unhook it once you tell me how to fly it. It's been in there for a good while now; a little longer won't hurt it any more than it already has been. I'd say that's rather fair."

"It only answers to Prince Ali," said Jasmine. "Whatever you say to it won't work."

"Can we dispense with the protests and indignation and just accept the situation we're in?" Abbas rolled his eyes. "How about you go on and tell me what to do? Is there a magic word or something to get it up? A way I'm supposed to hold the carpet?"

Ali crossed his arms and glared at the man.

"Okay, then." The man shrugged. "We tried it the nice way. Now let's do it my way."

Abbas raised his lamp and dangled it over the carpet. The fire flickered over the glass enclosing, dangerously close.

"What are you doing?" Jasmine cried out. She watched as the rug struggled once again to break free of the man's tight grip. The lantern was so hot that its proximity alone was making the magic carpet begin to smolder.

"If it won't work for me as you say," Abbas said loudly, "then it won't work for anyone, including the two of you. But I suggest that if you don't want to watch your little friend transform into a heap of smoke and ash, you come up with a way to help it change its mind. Otherwise, we're all going to have a sad little ending tonight, won't we?"

Jasmine's eyes widened as she saw the smoke increase.

This man was not bluffing. He was going to destroy the carpet.

They had to do something. Before it was too late.

Aladdin

Chapter Twenty

"GET THAT LANTERN away from the carpet!" Aladdin shouted at Abbas. He took a step toward the rug, but the man only smiled and lowered his lamp closer. Dark plumes now flowed from the carpet's center and Aladdin's eyes widened when he saw what looked to be an orange flicker catch upon the fabric.

"Careful there," Abbas warned. His hands were full. The carpet was tucked under one arm, the lantern hanging from the other and pressing against the rug. "It's best not to provoke a man like me who has nothing at all to lose. Take another step forward and I'll just take the glass clear off this lantern; won't be any question of what happens next to this pile of thread and cloth. The sea is too far below for you to even have any hope of putting it out."

"It won't listen to you," Aladdin said through clenched teeth. "I am its master. That's just how it's built."

"Then *tell* it to listen to me!" Abbas shouted. "It's a stupid rug; just order it to listen."

"It's not stupid," Jasmine interceded angrily. "And it will know anything he tells it to do will be because you're making him."

"I'm sure your friend here could be persuasive if he really wanted to be," Abbas said. "Seems he doesn't want to."

Aladdin took a step toward the man.

"Not another move," Abbas warned. "I may not know how this thing works, but I do know how fire operates." The carpet bucked and squirmed harder and harder. Its tassels shook wildly.

"Please!" Jasmine cried out. More smoke floated from

the carpet's body, and then Abbas leaned down and blew out the flame.

"That was just a preview," the man told them. "Let me know when you're ready to stop torturing this innocent thing because you'd rather keep it to yourself than save its life."

Aladdin glanced over at Jasmine. She looked as shaken as he felt. Abbas was right. The carpet was innocent. It hadn't done a thing to anyone, and now Abbas had burned it with his lamp.

Suddenly Aladdin's eyes widened. He knew what he had to do.

"Fine." Aladdin held up his hands up in a show of surrender. "You win. I'll help you get the carpet to follow your orders." He felt Jasmine's eyes settling on him, the question lingering on her lips.

"That's a sudden shift." The man raised an eyebrow. He lowered the lamp away from the carpet. "Go on, then. What do I need to do?"

"Flying a magic carpet is trickier than you think. Especially when it doesn't want to go with you in the first place. And now that you've burned it, it's going to make the task even more complicated. But the first step is to stop hurting it. You have to unhook it."

"Nice try." The man laughed. "You want me to unhook it, and then it'll just fly away."

"Do you want his help or not?" Jasmine interrupted. "As long as it is tethered, it can't get airborne. It's simple as that."

"And you're telling me this thing won't buck and run away?"

"Not if I tell it not to," said Aladdin. He took a tentative step forward toward Abbas, trying not to let his fury show at the burn straight down carpet's center. "Hey, buddy," he called out to the carpet. It was steps away from him now. "Listen, I know you're scared, but don't worry. Everything will be just fine, I promise. He's going to take that metal thing out of you, but once he does you have to not make a break for it. Do you trust me?"

At Aladdin's words, the magic carpet stopped fighting and went limp. Aladdin's heart broke a bit. Even in the Cave of Wonders where they had met one another not so long ago, when he'd seen it trapped, as it had been for so many hundreds of years—even then, Aladdin had not seen it look this defeated.

The man yanked the hook out of the carpet's body.

"Much better." Abbas nodded as he looked at the carpet's defeated form. "Thought my arm was going to fall off with all that kicking and bucking. It's stronger than it looks."

Aladdin looked at Jasmine's stricken expression and glanced back down at the carpet's gaping wound; it probably couldn't have flown now even if it had wanted to.

"Let's get on with it." The man tapped his foot. "What's next?"

"Now you say the magic words."

"Aha." The man smirked. "I knew there had to be some magic words."

"You got me," Aladdin said. "But you must say them in the right order. It's the only way. It's sort of like hypnotizing it. Once you have it under your spell, it's yours."

"Well, go on, then. What do I need to say?" Abbas glanced down at the rug and then back at Aladdin.

"It's a long sequence," Aladdin told him. "That's why I keep it written down." He turned to Jasmine and pointed to the map rolled up in her hands.

"That is quite the scroll." The man frowned. "Just how many words are there?"

"It's a magic carpet you're trying to operate. It's not going to be as simple as saying 'abracadabra.' If it were that easy, anyone could enchant and take it." He turned to Jasmine. "Go ahead and give him the scroll."

"Ali! No!" Jasmine played along and clutched the rolled-up map close to herself.

"Please, Jasmine. Come on." Aladdin reached his hand out. "We don't want this man to hurt the magic carpet any more. We'll figure out another way home."

Reluctantly, Jasmine handed Aladdin the rolled-up map.

"Well, say the words slowly and no funny business, understand?" the man said.

Aladdin held out the scroll to the man.

"I said you're a comedian, didn't I? What are you handing me that thing for? You know I can't hold that while I've got this carpet and lantern in my arms," the man snarled. "Read the words to me and I'll repeat after you."

"You have to read the words yourself. If I say them, the magic carpet will hear me first, and then it will listen to me."

"That's ridiculous." The man eyed the scroll suspiciously.

"I didn't make the rules." Aladdin shrugged. "Do you want control of the magic carpet, or don't you?" He held the paper out toward the man.

The man stared at it in the darkness, then looked down at the carpet under one arm and the lantern in the other. Grudgingly, he lowered the lantern safely to the ground beside him.

"Well, go on, then. What're you waiting for? Hand it over," he growled and took a step forward. He thrust out his hand.

It was now or never. Abbas took another step toward Aladdin. And then, Aladdin dove, rushing Abbas as hard as he could. He charged at him with his entire body. Abbas's eyes widened. He yelped as he lost his balance on the slippery terrain. Before he could recover, Aladdin yanked the carpet out from under his arm. The man stumbled as he tried to get up and fell again onto the ground with a thump.

Aladdin tucked the carpet under his arm, but before he could run, the man lunged. He tackled Aladdin's leg.

Aladdin fell to the ground with the carpet still wrapped tightly in his arms. Just then Aladdin saw the glint of metal. Abbas pulled out his knife. Aladdin rolled away, and the knife narrowly missed his torso. He ducked as the knife swung over his head.

"You think it's that easy to get one over me?" Abbas yelled, marching toward him. Aladdin's eyes widened. Behind him were the jagged cliffs, and in front of him was the man with the raised knife heading straight for him. But suddenly, Abbas's eyes widened. He fell to the ground, then visibly winced and cried out.

Aladdin straightened to see Jasmine smiling at him, her foot stuck out.

"Whoops." She raised an eyebrow.

The man writhed on the ground and howled in pain. Aladdin could see blood dripping from his knee. The knife was on the ground next to him, bloody. He'd cut himself.

Aladdin looked at Jasmine. "Run!" he shouted.

With the carpet under his arm, they raced through the boulders and down the gravel road, toward the kingdom. The golden minarets loomed in the distance.

"How far away is he, you think?" Jasmine asked. "He

was injured, but I don't think that wound is going to stop him from coming after us."

Before Aladdin could reply, they heard a bellowing shout.

"Where is he?" Aladdin wondered as they picked up their pace.

"Hard to say." Jasmine glanced about. There were caves all about them.

"At least he can't run too fast now." But with the carpet in his arms, Aladdin knew that their own pace was slower than it could have been. The injured magic carpet was heavier than he'd imagined. "We just have to make it back to the city. Once we're there, we're safe again."

"But can we really outrun him? He'll know all the shortcuts out here, at least better than us."

Aladdin's pace faltered. She was right. They couldn't risk getting caught. Not when the carpet was in no position to fly. And they had no weapons. Their best chance for safety was to evade him. Footsteps echoed in the distance now.

Aladdin spotted a large cave ahead. "There!" He

pointed. It was dark and big enough to fit all three of them. "Let's wait him out."

Jasmine followed his gaze. "Are you sure? What if he peeks inside and finds us?"

Just then they heard the crunch of gravel nearby.

They ducked into the cave and were instantly enveloped in complete darkness.

"I know you're hiding here somewhere." Abbas's voice floated close to them now. "Don't hear your footsteps anymore, but you can't be on the main road yet."

In the darkness, Aladdin reached out and took Jasmine's hand in his. She squeezed it and moved closer to him. He doubted the wisdom of slipping into a cave now. Perhaps they should have just kept heading toward the kingdom and hoped to simply outrun him. It was only a matter of time before Abbas peeked in and found them.

"Could we fly it back to Agrabah from this cave?" Jasmine whispered. "I know the carpet is injured, but even if it can just manage to take us to a nearby island, we will be safer than we are here."

He looked down at the carpet, and though the darkness concealed its exact appearance, Aladdin could feel it writhe in his arms.

"The damage from the burn was bad," Aladdin said. "I could see right through its center straight to the ground. And the hook didn't help matters, either. It can't take us anywhere with the way it is now."

The sound of crunching gravel grew closer.

"I was only going to take the carpet and be on my way," the man shouted. "But now I'm going to have to make you both pay personally for this. Stabbed myself in the knee and gashed an elbow on a rock when I fell. Someone's got to be accountable for that. I know these caves like the back of my hand. Don't worry. I will find wherever you're hidden. I've got all night."

Aladdin's stomach sank. What was he going to do when the man inevitably found them? They were boxed in now.

"Hey," Jasmine whispered all of a sudden. "It's the spider."

Aladdin was about to ask her what spider she was referring to, but there it was—in the dark of night, the glittering black creature perched at the edge of the cave's opening. It was Genie! Or rather, it was Genie the spider. In all that had transpired, Aladdin had nearly forgotten about the lagoon they had visited and the form he had taken when he met Jasmine. It almost felt like a life-time ago.

"What's he doing here?"

"I'm not sure," Aladdin said. Was Genie here to give them a message? Or were things so bad that Genie had come to forcibly make him use his wish? But the spider wasn't paying any attention to either of them as they spoke. Instead it was perched at the top of the cave's opening, spinning thread across the entrance.

"It's . . . I think it's building a web."

Jasmine was right! Aladdin watched with fascination as the glittering spider Genie wove a web, thick and dark, covering the entire opening of the cave in a matter of seconds.

"How did he do it so quickly?" Jasmine whispered. "It looks dusty."

"He's protecting us," Aladdin said, realizing what was occurring. "With a web that old-looking still intact, Abbas will walk right by without glancing in; he'll think we can't possibly have gotten in here without disturbing it!"

Moments later, the spider had finished, and the cobweb looked so thick Aladdin could hardly see through it.

Not more than fifteen seconds passed before they heard Abbas's heavy breathing. They saw his outline through the thick veil of cobweb as he walked past them. A trail of scarlet-red blood dripped to the ground with each step he took. Jasmine and Aladdin scooted their backs against the cool interior of the cave wall and sat absolutely still until, at last, he was gone.

"Come out, come out, wherever you are!" the man shouted out as he continued walking. "You can run, but you can't hide. I'll find you!" Abbas carried on, his voice growing more and more distant.

They were safe. Aladdin felt nearly giddy with relief.

"Thanks, pal," Aladdin whispered to the spider. "You saved us."

"Hey," hissed the spider in Aladdin's ear. "I did this for the carpet. It was my friend for centuries while we wasted away in the Cave of Wonders. It didn't do anything to deserve any of this. I wasn't going to let anyone hurt it."

"Fair enough," Aladdin whispered, and for the first time in a long time, he exhaled. Then, "He's probably heading toward town," Aladdin said to Jasmine.

"We don't need to go back that way, do we?" Jasmine asked.

"No," said Aladdin. "And once the townspeople find him wandering around there, they'll capture him anyway. The guards will make sure to lock him up."

"Good." Jasmine breathed out a sigh of relief.

"Let's take a look at you, Carpet," Aladdin said, gently patting the rug. "Let's see how bad your injury is."

With the time in the cave, their eyes had adjusted to the darkness, and they looked at the rug.

"How bad is it?" Jasmine asked Aladdin.

"He's definitely injured, but it might not be too bad," Aladdin said. "The singe is a straight line, at least. Maybe I can get it stitched up. Can I have your hairpin?" he asked Jasmine. At the same time, he pulled his hat off and yanked out threads from inside it.

"Thanks," he said as she handed him her pin.

"Will the string from your hat work on a magic carpet?" she asked.

"It's not the perfect solution," he admitted. "But it's better than nothing." He quickly got to work weaving the pin in and out of Carpet's body; in no time there was a tight stitch right through its center.

"All done." Aladdin handed Jasmine back the hairpin. "How do you feel, buddy?" he asked the magic rug.

The carpet stretched and straightened out and then shook itself from head to toe. A flurry of gold sparks flew about, and then, just like that, the center stitches vanished and the carpet looked good as new! It fluttered and zoomed from one end of the cave to the other, did a cartwheel, and then stretched to its full length and waved.

"Easy there." Aladdin laughed. "Don't overdo it. You only just got healed, and we have a long journey home."

"Thank you so much." Jasmine turned to the spider perched by the edge of the cave. The spider curtsied and then skittered off into the dark night.

Together they pushed aside the cobweb Genie had made; it parted like a velvet curtain. The carpet hovered next to them.

Aladdin looked at Ababwa in the distance. He was going to miss this place, but he would treasure the memories for the rest of his life. It was time to go home.

Jasmine

Chapter Twenty-One

"**Y**OU SURE you can get us back to Agrabah? You've been through a lot," Ali said to the carpet as they stood on the gravel road just outside the cave.

"He's right," Jasmine said. "It's a long journey home. If you need some time to recuperate, we'll understand."

The carpet zipped straight into the air and somersaulted twice before diving back to earth with a twirl.

"Okay. Okay. We get it." Ali laughed. "You're good as new, you show-off." He hugged the carpet, and though it couldn't make facial expressions, Jasmine could have sworn the rug looked happy.

The magic carpet rolled flat and hovered just above the ground now, ready to take Jasmine and Ali away. They were about to sit down when they heard someone shout.

"Wait!"

It was a little voice. Jamaal. He hurried toward them with a big smile.

"That was amazing!" the boy exclaimed. "I saw the whole thing. I couldn't believe it!"

"You were following us?" Ali asked in dismay.

"Sorry." The boy blushed. "But I had to see if you both were okay. It took me a while to find you, but when I finally caught up, I saw him coming at you with the knife! I got so scared I couldn't move."

"You did the right thing. You shouldn't have moved," Ali said quickly.

"But wow!" Jamaal clapped his hands. "The way you swerved and ducked! And then you rushed him! He didn't even see it coming!" He mimicked the way Ali had maneuvered away from Abbas's knife. "And then, Princess Jasmine, you tripped him! You knew exactly where to stand to send him tumbling to the ground! I can't believe

I got to meet not only a prince and a princess in person, but real live heroes too!"

Jasmine recognized that look of wonder in his eyes. It was the same expression she'd often had when she'd watched her mother resolving issues with ease and grace. Her father stressed about every problem that arose; it was part of the reason, she suspected, that he relied on Jafar as much as he did. But the effortless and calm way her mother had solved problems was almost a sort of magic unto itself.

"You're so sweet," Jasmine said. "But really, if anyone is a hero here, it's you."

"Me?" The boy looked at her and then at Ali, confused.

"Of course," Ali said. "If it wasn't for you, we wouldn't have even known how to find that man and the carpet. Your insight led us straight to him. Otherwise, who knows how long it would have taken us? Thank you for all your help."

"Oh." Jamaal's cheeks flushed a bit. "Um, you're welcome. I'm glad I could help. But I'm just a street rat up to no good. That's what everyone says, anyhow."

"Hey, that's not true," Ali said. "Don't accept the labels people put on you. You are no street rat. No matter where you live or your life's circumstances, you are still worthy." Ali kneeled down until he was eye to eye with the boy. "I know it's easy to believe the terrible things people say, even if what they're saying isn't true. I know what it's like to feel unworthy."

"You?" The boy's eyes narrowed with skepticism.

"Appearances can be deceiving," he said gently. "And I know you can't see a better life for yourself than the one you have now, but that doesn't mean it's not possible. Because I see the person you are. You've had a tough life. You've had to fend for yourself when you should have had someone looking after you. But those difficulties make you stronger and more resilient. You define yourself through your actions, not anyone's opinion of you."

Jasmine watched the way Ali spoke to the boy. The way his dimple deepened. How he truly *did* seem to understand what the boy was going through.

Any doubts she had vanished.

Prince Ali *had* to be the boy from the market she'd met. The person who had captured her heart. Nothing else made sense. It *had* to be him. But this made no sense at all. How could the boy from the streets with his charming pet monkey, Abu, also be the prince of Ababwa? And if he *was* the same person, why had he not said anything to her about it?

She watched the tender way Ali spoke to Jamaal. Now wasn't the time to bring it up. But she would definitely ask him about it later. She was not sure why she didn't feel upset about his not being fully honest with her. Maybe it was because after having spent so much time with him and seeing how gently he spoke to Jamaal now, she trusted he had a good reason for doing so. He had not let her down so far.

"It's time for us to get going," Ali told the young boy.

"Aw, really?" Jamaal's expression dropped. "So soon?"

"Unfortunately, it is," Jasmine told the boy. "But meeting you has definitely been one of the highlights of my time here."

"Thank you for forgiving me," he told the princess. "I am making you a necklace. I was working on it on the rooftop earlier this evening. I'm halfway done. Maybe next time Prince Ali visits, I can give it to him to give to you—or maybe you will come visit us again and I can give it to you myself."

"I would love that. Thank you." Jasmine smiled.

Jamaal moved to say something else, but suddenly

there was a loud crash. The boy's expression went from a smile to shock as he was wrenched backward.

Jasmine gasped.

Abbas.

No one had noticed him sneaking toward them from atop the boulder behind them, not until he had leapt down and grabbed the boy. Not until it was too late.

"Nice trick you played on me back there," Abbas said through ragged breaths. The boy was firmly in his clutches, his sharp blade resting against the boy's jugular now. "Should've known what you were up to. Clever ploy with that rolled-up map." He glared at them. "But I know better now."

"Abbas! No!" Ali shouted. "Please. Don't harm the boy. He didn't do anything to deserve any of this!"

"Deserve? What does that even mean? As though I deserve to be here?!" shouted Abbas. "You only deserve what you're foolish enough or smart enough to get."

"Look," Ali said quickly. "Here, you want the carpet? I'll show you how to use it now. It'll do what you want it to. No games. I swear it."

"Like I would believe you now?" Abbas sneered. "You think I'm *that* much of a fool?"

He turned to Jasmine.

"You," he said. "Any idea how this thing works?"

"I don't," Jasmine said quickly. "I swear it."

"Well, if neither of you can help me get off the ground and away from this godforsaken place, then I guess this boy can just say goodbye."

"Wait!" Jasmine cried out. "Give me a minute. Please, let me think."

She looked at the man's silvery white hair. She thought of the story she had read about this man. The way he had tried to turn the entire world against his own sultan because he wished to mine and extract the gold and silver beneath their mountainous region.

Jasmine had wondered what happened to that man from the legendary tale, for the story had simply ended when his life's work, the map of buried treasures, went up in flames. But now, she knew. She was looking directly at what his punishment had been: a lifetime in a remote prison in the outcroppings of undeveloped Ababwa. Even now, after all this time, he was still the sort of man who thought he knew best. Many such men in Abbas's position did—men who had never heard the word "no" in their lives.

CHAPTER TWENTY-ONE

"The Akbar family deserved to rule Sulamandra," Jasmine said.

The man jerked over to look in her direction. Jasmine tried not to wince at the look of sheer terror in the little boy's eyes. The blade was still pressed against the boy's neck—one wrong move, even an accident, and the man could harm that boy irreparably.

"What was that?" he asked.

"The Akbar family. That's your family name, isn't it?"

Her confidence grew as he perked up at this recognition. While Ali had thrown her for a loop with how different he was from the men she'd known all her life, she had had a lifetime of experiences with vain, self-congratulatory men like Abbas. Which meant she also knew the way to get to his weakness.

"I remember my mother talking about you all those years ago," Jasmine invented. "She had said it was such a tragedy what happened. Her kingdom was going to help you, of course."

"Yes, I'm sure they were." The man rolled his eyes. "No one helped me. Many things about that time are fuzzy, but I remember this well."

"We had no time to help you," Jasmine explained.

"The artillery you requested? The cannons? We had them all ready to load onto our boats. We were gathering the forces and armor you had asked for as well. But by the time we were ready to dispatch our ships, word came to us about the tragedy of the fire. That it was all too late. And then of course no one had any idea where you had gone to."

"Yes." The man's eyes darkened. "That's why he banished me the way he did."

"It wasn't right," Jasmine said. "I'm sure he didn't even give you a chance to explain your side of the situation, did he? We would have sent people to come and rescue you had we known where you'd been sent. You were wronged."

"Exactly." The man's eyes widened and he nodded his head vigorously. "Sultan Waleed gave me no opportunity to defend myself. A quick overnight trial—if you can even call it that—when everyone there was his loyalists and pawns . . . So you understand." He looked at her.

"I do."

"Then you know exactly why I need to leave," he said. "I can't let them get away with what they've done."

"Of course. From one royal to another, they must pay

for what they did to you. You absolutely must right this grave injustice."

She could feel Ali's eyes on her; he was surely wondering what she was up to. But she had to stay focused. This time, Ali would have to be the one to trust her.

"But what I am genuinely confused about," she continued, "is why you would want to take a shaky, unreliable carpet; it's singed from the lantern and injured. And the hook you had in it seems to have messed with its sense of direction. For all you know, it could end up dropping you in the middle of the Sahara with the way it's functioning right now."

"What else can I do?" Abbas asked. "I have to try whatever way I can to leave this blasted place. Better this rug than no option at all."

"Well, how about something stronger and more solid, with a lot more reliability?"

"Such as?"

"A boat," she said.

"You think I haven't tried that?" he scoffed. "Weren't you listening when I told you that I've tried leaving this awful place by sea? The waves cut into any vessel I try to build like knives."

"I'm not talking about a raft. I'm talking about a ship. A seafaring one."

"Like I'd get on any of *those ships* out there. As if *they're* going to get me anywhere," the man spat.

"Do you mean the one with the white mast that came in this morning?" Jamaal cried out. "But that's your ship, Princess Jasmine. You'd give him *that* one? The one with all that gold in it?"

"Jamaal," Jasmine admonished, pretending to be flustered.

"Sorry," the boy said. "I was curious and snuck in when I was certain that the captain was asleep. I didn't steal anything, I swear it. But there was *so* much gold."

"I'm sure you didn't take anything," Jasmine said. "But." She turned to the villain and pretended to consider. "I can give *you* some of the gold. God knows my kingdom has plenty of it."

"You're trying to get me to believe that one of those ships out there is yours?" The man snorted. "And you'll just give me a literal boatload of gold?"

"As well as a captain to steer the boat for you."

"Jasmine!" Ali exclaimed. "Your father will be furious."

"Ali, let me sort this out myself, thank you." She gave him her best haughty glance and turned back to Abbas.

"And you would do all of that why?" he asked. "From the goodness of your heart?"

"Because if those of royal worthiness do not protect one another, who will?" she asked. "My mother meant to send ships to assist you before everything unfolded with the fire and your banishment. Allow me to give you one ship now as a gesture of goodwill. It's what she would have wanted. It's not a tough decision to me. Why would anyone go back on a flimsy rug when you can go back to the kingdom that is rightfully yours with a ship, crew, captain, and enough gold to actually exact your revenge? Money is, after all, power. And *that* is how you make a comeback. What sort of vengeance does a man in tattered clothing take with a simple rug like this?"

"All this to protect this peasant boy?" Abbas frowned.

"I don't want to see him hurt. He's only a child." Jasmine nodded. "But my decision to help you is strategic. Allow me the chance to help you, and maybe one day you will be grateful enough to form an alliance with Agrabah, as we had meant to do long ago."

"A boat full of gold? You'll just give me that to form an alliance?" Abbas asked suspiciously.

"Isn't Sulamandra full of gold?" Jasmine countered. "If you go back home and defeat Sultan Waleed, then you'll be swimming in gold and silver, won't you? Those mountains will be all yours to mine, won't they? Surely you'll repay Agrabah for helping you during your time of need. There is no downside for my kingdom to assist you."

"Maybe . . ." Abbas considered Jasmine's offer.

"Jasmine," Ali said. "Your father . . ."

"My father will be pleased we were able to lend our assistance to such an important man," Jasmine retorted. "Please allow us to rectify the tragic mistake."

Abbas smiled. His yellow teeth looked like a string of corn.

"Fine," he finally said. "Go summon the captain and bring proof of this wealth that is in that boat you speak of. If you can prove what you say is true, we have a deal."

"I can do that." She nodded. "In the meantime, can't you put the boy down? Holding him like that means even a slight accidental turn risks his life."

"Accidents happen." He kept his grip firmly on the

boy and shrugged. "You have one hour. But bear in mind that after the ordeal back at the cliffs, my patience is growing thin. If you're not back in time"—he looked down at Jamaal, his expression darkening—"this boy is dead."

Aladdin

Chapter Twenty-Two

ALADDIN WATCHED Jasmine disappear around the curve into the distance. The blade Abbas held was still balanced precariously close to the little boy's throat. Aladdin had ducked and fled from people like Abbas all his life. He knew how arrogant they were, how they thought their wealth afforded them the right to treat anything and anyone as they pleased. They didn't see people like Aladdin himself as actual people. Aladdin also knew something else: a man like this was not bluffing. If they didn't come up with a solution to save Jamaal, Abbas would murder the boy.

Jamaal's not actually real, Aladdin reminded himself. *He's a figment of Genie's conjuring.* And yet, when he looked at Jamaal now, his green eyes wide, tears trailing his cheeks, the boy felt as real as anyone Aladdin had ever known.

Aladdin studied the winding path Jasmine had taken just a little while earlier and wondered what he could do. He knew what Abbas didn't know. There were no royal boats from Agrabah docked at the pier. There was no gold. No captain. Jasmine had said what she needed to in order to buy them some more time to figure out a solution, but as the clock ticked and the minutes passed, he wondered what to do before Abbas carried out his threat.

A patch of clouds passed over the moon, concealing it completely. The darkness felt as though it had settled into his own heart as well.

"I must admit it took me a while to figure out what you were up to," Abbas told Aladdin. "But I get it now. She's a pretty one, isn't she?"

"Don't talk about her," Aladdin snapped.

"Been trying to figure out what the heck was going on with this ridiculous kingdom. When I first saw the burst of light flickering in the darkness, I thought I was finally losing my mind. And then watching a palace spring up on this godforsaken land out of nowhere . . . Are you a wizard or something? A genie? Some can be impressed with that sort of thing, that's for sure. But I know of that girl's father—he won't ever approve of her running off with an illusionist like yourself. You're new money. Can smell it a mile away." He wrinkled his nose.

"You don't know anything about me."

"But still, credit where credit is due. This is indeed quite the dog and pony show you have going on here," Abbas continued. "And I would wager my family's entire wealth that she has no idea at all who you really are. But I know. You're a fake and a fraud. You're not a prince. You're a nobody."

The words landed like rocks in the well of Aladdin's heart. He swallowed. The man was evil and cruel, but he was right. Except for one thing—Aladdin wasn't old or new money. He truly was nobody.

"Prince Ali is a hero!" Jamaal shouted. "He was kind

to me and helped me and he's braver than you'll ever be."

"Who asked for your input?" Abbas snapped at the boy.

Aladdin felt sick. Abbas was getting in his head.

"You remind me so much of him, you know that?" Abbas told Aladdin. "You and Waleed could have been long-lost brothers. He was also a do-gooder who thought if he just got everyone to like him, he'd be the best or win some kind of a medal. But he was a nobody, too. Even with a crown and parents with blue-blooded lineage, it doesn't mean anything if you're weak willed and cowardly. You know everything I'm saying is the truth. I can tell you understand exactly what I'm telling you." He peered into Aladdin's eyes. "Are you afraid I'll point out that inconvenient matter about who you really are to your companion? I don't need to tell her. If your pretty princess doesn't see it now, she will. It's only a matter of time. She is no fool."

Aladdin looked down at the ground. His head hurt. His chest ached. Abbas was a power-crazed egomaniac.

But he was also right.

Aladdin was no prince. And he was certainly not worthy of a woman as lovely and wonderful and intelligent as Jasmine. Sooner or later the truth about who he really was would come out. There was no way around that.

He looked at the boy in Abbas's clutches.

The only way to prove himself worthy of a woman like Jasmine was to *be* worthy of her. Not with a brilliant palace or fancy clothing. Truly worthy. The only way to do that was to go back home and earn his worth fair and square.

He looked out into the darkness; he wondered where Jasmine had gone. If he couldn't come up with a solution, could she?

Jasmine

Chapter Twenty-Three

JASMINE HAD never run so fast in her life. She raced down the road, perspiration tinging her brow, her insides clenched. But she didn't stop until she had left the overgrown road behind her, passed the docks with the boats lolling silently in the night, and at last stepped onto the familiar cobblestoned streets of Ababwa. Only then did she let out a gasp and steady herself, but only for a moment. All she had to do was think of the boy, the way his entire body trembled, his hands limp at his sides as the man gripped him by the neck, and she'd push on, past her exhaustion. Jasmine continued until she reached the village square.

Despite the late hour, a handful of people still milled about outside. A few held torches with lit flames while others carried lanterns. When they saw her, they hurried toward her.

"Princess Jasmine! Are you all right?" a man asked.

"Thank you, all of you, for being up so late, for helping us." Jasmine exhaled. "I need to talk to you all. It's urgent."

"We've scoured every inch of the kingdom," a woman said. "There's no sign of the thief or the carpet you are looking for. But don't worry, we won't stop looking."

"There's no need for that," said Jasmine as a crowd gathered around her. "We found the man. He doesn't have the carpet anymore, but he's taken Jamaal hostage. He's got a knife to the boy's throat and threatens to kill him within the hour."

The crowd gasped audibly.

"Where is he?" Zaria asked, her jaw clenched. Her gilded cage was cradled against her arm. "I'll sic my bees on that man. These friends of mine here make good honey, but they also know how to attack like the best of their species."

"Thank you," Jasmine said. "The bees may come in handy."

"Well, what are we waiting for?" The bread maker raised his torch. "Let's go and get him." Others nodded and murmured in agreement.

"He's by the cliffside," Jasmine said. "Ahmed calls it the Phoenix Trio."

At this, the crowd fell silent.

"Did you say the Phoenix Trio?" a woman finally asked. "But that place is uninhabitable. No one goes out there. Not ever."

"Perhaps that's why he fled there; he thought no one would think to go there," Jasmine said. "But we really must leave at once. We don't have a moment to lose."

The townspeople exchanged worried glances.

"Princess," a man finally said, hesitantly, "we would like to help—we would. And we are sorry for Jamaal. Truly, we are. But none of us knows how to travel to those cliffs."

"They're dangerous," a woman called out. "The water crashing against the cliffs makes the land slippery."

"And in the dark, it's all too simple to slip to one's death."

"But if we can't help him, who will? He's only a child!" Jasmine said, astonished.

"We aren't proud of how we feel, Princess. We are good people. Really, we are. And we feel for the boy, but he also knew how dangerous those cliffs were."

Jasmine couldn't believe what she was hearing. During her brief time in Ababwa, these villagers had been kind and giving to her and Ali. And yet they were willing to let their fear overtake their compassion? They would let Jamaal die?

"I know it's dangerous," Jasmine said. "But think of Sultan Zayn the tenth. What kingdom have his wise words not reached?" she asked them. "Remember what he said about matters such as this? Did he not say that while the world is filled with kind and good people, the only way we can see a kind and good world is if we look beyond ourselves and intercede to help others when we can? If we don't help Jamaal, he will die. And no one deserves a death like this."

"She's right," said Zaria, taking a step forward. She looked over at the crowd. "He's no different from Maha's little boy, or any of our children in this kingdom . . . or us. We were all small and helpless once, too, weren't we? He made a mistake going out there, he did. But with no parents to shade his path, it is we who must help him. If it were our own children out there, we would go in an instant."

"I'm sorry I was callous," one of the men said. "It's been a tough few weeks in the kingdom. Our energies are a bit spent."

"I understand," said Jasmine. "Let us be judged tonight not on the words we said but on the actions we took. Will you help me?"

"Yes," said the bread maker.

"Yes," said Zaria.

"Yes!" shouted everyone, and Jasmine looked and realized the crowd had grown significantly. Every man, woman, and child from Ababwa stood straight at attention.

"Thank you." She breathed a sigh of relief. "Now let's save Jamaal."

Aladdin

Chapter Twenty-Four

"**Y**OUR PRINCESS is taking her sweet time," mused Abbas. "Unlike you, I am a man of my word, and I will make good on my promise."

Aladdin had no way to know what time it was or how much of it had passed, especially when each second felt like it lasted a lifetime.

And despite that, Aladdin was no closer to figuring out what he could do to save the boy and get out of Ababwa. Jamaal's tears had stopped by now, salty and dried against his cheeks, as though he'd begun to accept his fate.

"Look, do you want the secret to the carpet's magical ways or don't you?" Aladdin tried yet again. "I will give them to you this time. You have my word."

"Your word, eh? We both know what your word is worth."

"It's me you're angry with," Aladdin said, changing tactics. "Let me take the boy's place. If she doesn't come back in time, punish me. There's no reason to kill him. He hasn't done anything to you."

"I wonder what part of him I'll start with," Abbas mused. He acted as though Aladdin hadn't even said a word. Aladdin watched him wave his knife in the air. It glinted against the moonlight. "It's been a while since I've had any real fun. Perhaps we could start with the toes? The fingers? Maybe I'll have him decide. What say you, my friend?" He looked down at the boy and laughed.

Aladdin's fists tightened. His jaw clenched. He wanted nothing more than to storm over and shove this villain to the ground.

Abbas laughed at Aladdin.

"Want to strike me, don't you? I have to admit this wouldn't be nearly as much fun if you weren't here. Your reactions are priceless, truly." He glanced over his shoulder and then turned back to Aladdin. "You know there's always the possibility that she is not coming back. Maybe she ran off to save herself in that ship she'd promised me. Can't really blame her, can you? You and this waste of breath I've got under my arm aren't really worth fighting for, if we're being completely honest." He looked up at the moon and squinted. "I'd say we have another five minutes, give or take. It's a shame this has to end, though. After having only silverfish and the roaches for company all these years I was rather enjoying our chat, and I was most certainly looking forward to getting off this blasted place tonight. But no matter, whether it's tonight or tomorrow night or next month, I will get out sooner or later."

The boy started to struggle again, trying to kick against the man's torso. Abbas smacked him against the head. The boy winced and then fell silent. Soon Jamaal would have welts on his head where the man had struck him.

But the boy is not truly alive, Aladdin reminded himself yet again. Any bruise that he might sustain didn't actually count, did it? Even if Abbas were to follow through with his threat and kill Jamaal, it technically wouldn't be murder, because the boy had never existed to begin with. It didn't count.

Except it did. Because it all felt so real. And because all Aladdin could see when he looked at the little boy was himself, once upon a time. He also knew that even if the boy was not a real person, Aladdin *was*, and what he did or didn't do would matter to him and stay with him for the rest of his life.

Aladdin knew that there was one thing he could do. One thing that would undoubtedly save this boy's life and end all of this once and for all—a wish. He'd used one to become a prince, and he'd promised his final wish to free Genie. But there was still one more he could use. And though logically it felt preposterous to spend a wish on an imaginary boy, *his* choice to save him or not was a very real one. Aladdin wondered if he could reach into his satchel for the lamp without Abbas noticing.

"The first person I will kill when I get back home is the king, of course." Abbas looked off at the horizon thoughtfully. "Second try will have to be a charm. Next I'll go for the guards, the ones who locked me away. But they must suffer. I wouldn't have it any other way. I could set them loose in a meadow and hunt them. Now *that* could be fun." Abbas laughed. He continued with the list of revenge. It was time, Aladdin realized. It was time to put an end to all of this.

He moved his hands slowly toward the satchel to reach for the lamp buried within. He opened his mouth to whisper Genie's name. But before he could, he paused. There was a faint sound in the distance. Aladdin glanced at Abbas, but he was too busy rambling about his grand plans to notice. But Aladdin did. There, like a long and winding snake, was a line of people—the bread maker, the sweet vendor, the woman with the goats. Some carried torches while others carried lanterns. Practically the entire town was there. And leading them, at the front of the crowd—her face now visible to him in the distance— was Jasmine.

Jasmine

Chapter Twenty-Five

JASMINE MET ALI'S gaze as soon as she turned the bend. She watched his nervous expression shift from shock and disbelief to relief. She'd been nervous Abbas would see them coming down the pathway, but she needn't have been concerned; Abbas was so busy going on and on about something, his back turned to the walkway, he didn't notice Jasmine or the others as they drew closer. Soon she was mere steps away. She stared at his back. She could shove him—throw him off guard. But the man still held the knife close to the boy's jugular. It wasn't worth the risk.

"I'm back," she finally said.

Abbas stopped talking. He turned around with a smile. But his expression soured within seconds once he took in the crowd of people behind her.

"Should've figured," he grumbled.

"Perhaps," Jasmine said. "Everyone from Ababwa is here. Hurt the boy and there is no happy ending for you. But it doesn't have to come to that. The boy is all we care about. Let him go and no one needs to get hurt. Not even you."

"So generous of you." Abbas sneered. "But I'm afraid your little stunt is going to cost you. I told you I was going to kill this boy if you didn't bring me proof of the ship and the gold. So now this boy is going to die while you watch. I must say"—he shook his head—"royalty is really not what they say it is anymore. If you can't trust a royal with their word, who can you trust?"

"Don't!" Jasmine took a step forward; the crowd moved restlessly behind her. Abbas raised his knife.

"Please!" Jamaal shouted. "Have mercy."

"Mercy?" He looked down at the boy. "You do know none of this is my fault, don't you? All I wanted was that blasted magic carpet and a way out of here, but these people, your supposed protectors and friends, couldn't care less." He glared at both Ali and Jasmine. "Now they claim to want to save your life. It baffles me, quite frankly why they pretend as if they care. Because you're a nobody, kid. Sorry to say. Though I'm sure you knew that already. These townspeople here? They only came because a princess ordered them to. No one there cares a lick about you."

The boy's lower lip trembled.

"Don't listen to him," Jasmine told the boy. "If they didn't care, they wouldn't have come." She turned to Abbas. "People can change their perspectives. They can change their ways. Even *you* could change if you truly wanted to. Despite all that has happened and all that you have done, it's still not too late for you. You can still do the right thing, and you can start by letting this boy go."

"As if I'd listen to you. I make decisions and stick with them. I'm no weak fool."

"Changing one's mind doesn't make one a fool."

Jasmine turned to look at the townspeople, then looked back at Abbas. "If anything, it can be a sign of wisdom and strength."

"You ask for mercy for this boy, but has anyone shown *me* any mercy in my life?" Abbas asked. "Everyone has been on my case from the time I was born. I was to walk faster than any other boy, recite the poetry of the greats, and get slapped if I made so much as a small misstep. The only attention I got was from that weak-willed Waleed. That sort of love," he scoffed, "it doesn't even count. No. Mercy is not the way of the world. I've been wronged my whole life and now I am not going to be wronged ever again. . . ."

Abbas went on, listing all the ways he had been treated unjustly as a child and as a teenager. As Abbas's narrative approached his early adulthood, Jasmine knew the only thing that stood in the way of Jamaal's death was Abbas's love for speechifying. The boy seemed to understand this, too. He looked resigned. As though it were already done.

Jasmine glanced over at Zaria. Their eyes met. Jasmine nodded. It was time. Zaria slid a finger over the cage door and opened it. The bees emerged, hovering for a quick moment before darting out of their cage. They zoomed now, glittering black and gold against the night sky, toward Abbas.

Jasmine glanced at Ali. His eyes followed the movement of the bees. He didn't move a muscle.

Abbas could have noticed, too, had he paused in his monologue to pay attention to his surroundings. But perhaps because he'd had no captive audience for so long, he could not stop speaking, which gave Zaria and her bees the perfect opportunity.

"And when I get back to the kingdom that was meant to be mine and reclaim my former glory, I will come back for all of you!" he shouted. "You can be *my* subjects then. I'll make this pathetic little kingdom that sprouted from nothing into my colony. And I will remember how you all treated me while I was here. How you all stood ready to harm a man who will someday rule you. And that palace of yours, that ridiculous monstrosity, I will burn to the ground. Except this time, I'll do it on purpose," he cackled.

The bees were almost there.

Moments away.

And then—they attacked.

"Gahhhh!" Abbas's smug expression vanished. He

screamed at the top of his lungs. In an instant, he dropped his hands and cowered so as to cover his face. The boy fell hard to the ground. The knife Abbas had been holding clattered on a rock by their feet.

"Get off me!" screamed Abbas, batting his hands at the bees and crouching with his face to the ground. Zaria had been correct about them; those bees were not ordinary in any way. They continued to attack him with a vengeance, swarming his face in a glittering blur.

Ali rushed to the fallen child and scooped him and the knife up. The boy clutched the prince and burrowed his head into Ali's shoulder. Even from where Jasmine stood, she could see how Jamaal's entire body trembled.

"It's okay," Jasmine heard Ali tell the boy. "You're safe now. You're safe. I promise."

"Burn us to the ground, will you?" shouted the butcher.

Zaria snapped her fingers three times, and the bees retreated and slipped noiselessly back into their cage.

"Make us a colony, eh?" said another of the towns-people, advancing upon him.

"I didn't mean it *literally*, of course." Abbas cleared his throat. He slowly sat up. His face was bumpy and puffed from all the beestings there and on his neck and arms and legs. "Now if you'll excuse me."

He stood unsteadily on his feet and then tried to make a run for it, but before he could so much as take a single step, the butcher and others grabbed Abbas and gripped him firmly beneath the arms. Other villagers came over and grabbed a hold of each leg.

"Unhand me at once!" Abbas shouted. "You can't contain me. Go on and lock me up. I will just get out again. You'll see."

"Ah, perhaps." A villager grinned. "But won't it be fun to try?"

Jasmine watched as they carted Abbas off with him kicking and shouting the entire way.

"Where are they taking him?" Jasmine asked Ali as she watched the retreating procession.

"Prison," Ali said. "A sturdier one in town, where more eyes can make sure he doesn't escape. Thanks to you."

"It wasn't me. Those bees . . ."

"The bees were here because of you," Ali said gently. "If you hadn't brought everyone here to help us, I don't know what I would have done." He gazed at her. "You're incredible, you know that?"

Jasmine smiled. Whoever this person she stood across from in this moment was, whether Ali or the boy named Aladdin she'd met at the market, he was pretty incredible, too. She could never have imagined feeling the way she did right now for someone, but she was glad she had trusted him. She was glad she had taken the risk of going on this magic carpet ride with him. Even with the danger and all that had transpired, it had been worth it to be with him.

From *LEGENDARY LEADERS ACROSS THE AGES*—
"Sultana Amina, or: The Measure of Love"

SULTANA AMINA gazed out the palace window at the still blue lake across the meadow in the distance.

"Still doesn't feel like home, does it?" Ramy asked her.

"Not yet," she replied. "Each time I glance out, I expect to see my mountain ranges and to hear the roar of the sea beating against the cliffs. It's strange to no longer be in Moribania."

"We are in Moribania," he reminded her gently.

"True," she agreed. For indeed this new land was still

the kingdom of Moribania, simply relocated from their homelands that had recently been reduced to rubble by a terrible earthquake. "I think it will just take some getting used to seeing it that way."

"Give it time," Ramy said. "Time has a way of smoothing things over."

"Have you heard any complaints?" she asked him. "From people out and about? Any grumblings I should know about?"

"To the contrary." Ramy shook his head. "Now that the last of the shops is finally built and the free medical clinics are up and running, everyone is content once more. Don't worry so much, Amina," he said. "Everyone is fine."

"You always know the right thing to say," she said.

"I have a knack for that, don't I?" Ramy winked.

Amina smiled at Ramy. It was true. He did have a way of knowing just what to say and of helping the sultana see things in new ways. They'd grown up side by side since they were infants—he was her nanny's son, and she'd never known life without him. It was he who had helped her to at last decide to make the move from their ancestral lands of Moribania to the newly purchased safer lands. He was also one of the only people in her life who spoke plainly to her as a person and not with the formality and the hesitation of speaking to one of the most powerful leaders in the Eastern hemisphere.

"You seem preoccupied lately," Ramy said. "It seems to be more than just the move?"

"I don't know," she sighed. "It's just that with the kingdom finally secure and people at last settled, I wonder if it's time for me to begin to contemplate my own personal next steps."

"Marriage?" he asked.

"A strong alliance with another kingdom would be good for Moribania. Particularly after everything the people have been through."

"I'm certain you would have fifty suitors from the finest kingdoms lined up tomorrow if you let it be known you were interested in marriage."

"Perhaps," she agreed. "But I want more than a political alliance to strengthen Moribania's position in the world, as important as that is; I also wish to like the person I marry and connect with them on a personal level. I'm not sure someone like me can have it both ways."

"You'll think of something, Amina," Ramy said. "If I

know you as well as I think I do, you will find a way to have both." He smiled, lifted his duster, and walked out of the room.

Amina watched him leave and sighed. She knew a marriage filled with love and mutual understanding was a complicated matter when one was sultana of a kingdom many would be eager to make binding alliances with through matrimony. How to separate those who were genuine in asking for her hand, and those who simply wished to amass more power?

Just then her eye caught on the artwork framed beside a window overlooking the meadow. The piece was a simple enough canvas at first glance. A princess had gifted it to her recently during a diplomatic mission from her island kingdom, and Amina had loved it at first sight. It had a white background and two circles of paint, one blue and one a deep red, both dripping down into a swirl of purple.

And then, Amina's eyes widened. She knew what to do.

The next day a royal invitation was sent to all the lands near and far. Sultana Amina was interested in marriage, said the invitation. However, as a busy woman, she did not have time to engage in courtship with many people. Instead, suitors were invited to visit the palace to answer one simple question. If they answered correctly, the sultana and the suitor could proceed with conversation, courtship, and possibly marriage if both parties desired.

From the moment the invitations were sent, people from around the world arrived daily, eager to at last meet the famed sultana. Royals from kingdoms large and small, some new to her and others quite familiar, lined up before the palace doors. Ramy led each person in, one by one. He escorted them into the royal hall where the sultana sat on her throne, and he asked each person who came the same question.

"The sultana would like to know what you see in that canvas," he said, drawing the suitor's attention away from the sultana and toward the art on the wall.

Some who arrived simply stared at him, confused at the question. Others grew irate at the idea of such a ridiculous request. Still others tried to sweet-talk and sidestep the question altogether, asking the queen for a moment alone. But Amina would not speak to anyone until they had answered this question correctly.

The interpretations of what the artwork represented were wide and varied. Some thought the painting looked as though it had been printed with little fingers, and thus the artwork meant the queen wanted children—an heir for her throne. Others thought perhaps the sultana had painted the canvas herself, so they told her they saw within the canvas a most intelligent and beautiful creator. But try as they might, each person got it wrong and were sent on their way.

"Perhaps a different test?" Ramy suggested one evening after a record fifty-seven suitors came and went, all dejected.

"No." She shook her head firmly. "I compromise on so many things for the sake of my kingdom, but whom I spend my life with, I will choose on my own terms."

"I hope soon enough you will see who it is you were meant to find," Ramy said.

After many months passed, however, with not a single suitor close to guessing the truth behind the artwork, Karim, her advisor approached her, his expression tense.

"Forgive me, Sultana, but I must inform you that people are talking," he said. "They wonder if you are doing this test out of some sort of perverse amusement. You have earned a great deal of goodwill among your subjects and your advisors and council members, but this game of yours is making many wonder about your state of mind."

Amina watched him walk away. She kept her composure, but a flicker of worry rose within her. She knew her advisor did not mean to be harsh; he was entrusted to tell her the truth, keep his ear to the ground, and report back. If he had dared to tell her this so bluntly, the conversations had to be harsher than he was letting on. She wondered: was the advisor right? Was she truly asking for too much?

Her thoughts were interrupted by Ramy.

"It's the strangest thing, isn't it?" he said, staring at the canvas.

"What is?" she asked.

"How anyone cannot know what that painting is about. It's plain as day."

"You know what it means?" Amina asked cautiously. Though she trusted Ramy more than anyone else in her life, she had not told anyone what she had seen in the painting.

"Of course," he nodded. "The separate colors—the red and blue—they are rich and beautiful, and then"—he trailed a finger following how they merged and consumed one another—"they change into a wholly new color. Except that if you study it carefully enough, you know that there are specks of blue and red throughout the new shade. They are one color, and yet still their own colors. It's a portrait of love. Or at least, love as it should be—a union, but one that honors the best of both people."

Amina stared at Ramy.

Ramy. The man who had stood by her side all her life. The one who had helped her and counseled her. Who had never let her down. She could make so many good decisions and have so much insight about so many things—and yet, when it came to this, how could she not have seen? Why had she presumed she had to marry another royal for stability and security for her kingdom, when love was a greater stabilizer than a title or a person's financial worth?

"It's you," she said softly. "It always has been, hasn't it?"

Ramy looked at her. His eyes brimmed with tears.

"I had hoped one day you would see."

The next day, a beautiful, elaborate wedding was held on the grounds of the palace. And from that day on Sultana Amina and her husband ruled their kingdom together. The people who had privately doubted Amina's decision to marry Ramy understood with time that the union of two people who loved one another and helped one another reach new heights would only pass on its bounty and joy to their entire kingdom.

Aladdin

Chapter Twenty-Six

"*Y*OU SURE you're okay?" Aladdin asked Jamaal.

"It looked worse than it really was," the boy said. "I feel okay now."

Aladdin looked over the boy's arms and neck, but aside from some bruising by his shoulders, he did seem to be all right.

"Thank you," Jamaal told Aladdin and Jasmine as they walked toward the kingdom proper. They stepped onto the cobblestoned street and saw lights turning off in the homes they walked past. It had been a busy day; everyone was exhausted. Jamaal looked off to the side of the road. "It's strange to think about it, but he's here in this town right this minute. The jail is only a five-minute walk from right where we're standing. He got out of the other prison, didn't he? What if he gets out from this new one? What if he looks for me again?"

"He's locked up pretty securely now," Aladdin reassured him. "There's around-the-clock surveillance, too. I know it must still feel terrifying, but they won't let him out of their sight now. Not after all the insults he hurled and threats he made."

"Maybe they can banish him to another land," Jamaal said.

"That's not a bad idea," Aladdin said, with a pang of sadness—because there would be no need to banish this man anywhere else. This place would soon return to its deserted state of being, as it had been before Genie created Ababwa. He knew as soon as he and Jasmine sat on the magic carpet and left this city out of view, Ababwa would disappear along with the villagers, the palace, Ahmed's map shop, the cafés, and this boy, too. The prison that contained Abbas would also vanish, and he would be no worse off than before—banished in a desolate, uninhabited land, debating if he'd made up all that had transpired.

Aladdin almost wondered the same thing. Because the boy who stood in front of him felt as real as the earth beneath them, and yet he wasn't. Perception was a tricky thing.

"Do you want to hang out in my palace for a little while?" Aladdin asked him. "I won't be there, but the servants will treat you well, and you can pick any of the guest rooms you'd like to sleep in."

"Actually, Prince Ali," someone said.

They turned around to see Zaria, standing close by and watching. "I was going to ask if Jamaal would like to stay with me."

"You?" The boy's eyes widened.

"Yes." She nodded. "The princess's words from earlier got me thinking. What use is it to think of ourselves as good people when we don't look out for those who need us? And you deserve a home like any child does. In truth, I should have opened my home to you long ago."

"I don't need anyone's charity." Jamaal crossed his arms. "I do okay as is on the streets."

"This isn't charity, child," she said. "This would be a two-way street. You need a place to stay and someone to watch out for you. I need someone to apprentice for me. I am the last in my line. I have no heirs. To learn the way of keeping these bees is crucial for this kingdom. And now that Maha's making the awnings for my bees, there will be more again, too many for me to handle alone. Are you interested in giving it a trial run? In exchange, you can stay with me. You'll attend the nearby school, and you can have a roof over your head and food to eat. What do you say?"

"Okay," Jamaal agreed with a widening grin. "We could see how it goes. Sorry," he said, turning to Prince Ali. "I know your palace would be great, but it would be nice to learn a skill and all."

"I agree." Aladdin leaned down to give the boy a hug.

"You're going to do great," Jasmine told him.

"I hope I will *be* great one day," Jamaal said. "I know I'll never be great like you, Prince Ali, but even if I can't rule kingdoms, I hope I can be good at what I do."

"You don't need to rule people to be great," Aladdin told him. "Being a good person and working in the way of justice however you can—those are the things that the truly worthy do. I know it's the kind of person *I* still hope to be."

The boy smiled at Aladdin and Jasmine and then walked over to Zaria. The four of them waved goodbye, and Aladdin and Jasmine watched Jamaal and Zaria walked over to her home with the red painted door. She opened it, and the two of them went inside.

Aladdin turned to Jasmine, knowing they could no longer delay the inevitable. "Ready to go back to Agrabah?"

"It's time to go," she agreed.

The carpet hovered above the ground once more. Aladdin and Jasmine settled in, and together they floated into the sky, among the twinkling stars.

As they drifted away, Aladdin turned to watch Ababwa disappear from sight. Now that they could no longer see it, it was probably back to the desolate land it had once been. But at least for a brief time it had been his kingdom.

He knew it was an impossible dream, but as the carpet geared up to zip them back to Agrabah, Aladdin hoped he'd one day have the chance to visit this place again. Even if only in his dreams.

Jasmine
Chapter Twenty-Seven

$\mathcal{T}$HE GOLDEN minarets of Ababwa disappeared from view, and in mere seconds they zipped across cities, countries, and continents until they were back where it all began: in the kingdom of Agrabah. *Her* kingdom.

The magic carpet flew low now, close to the city. In the distance Jasmine saw a wedding, the celebrations carrying on well into the night. Candles and lanterns were lit, and people danced. Everyone's faces filled with joy.

It was almost as though the night they'd experienced

had been a dream they were only waking up from. But she glanced at Ali and smiled. Of course it hadn't been a dream. It had been one of the most authentic nights of her life. And though they had seen so many places . . .

"Out of all the places you've shown me, this is by far the most beautiful," Jasmine said, looking at the glimmering lights and the smiles on everyone's faces; the lanterns cast a warmth over the rest of Agrabah. And she realized as she said it that it was true. Sure, it wasn't as awe-inspiring as the thundering waterfalls overlooking misty jungles, or the quiet island with the bioluminescent fish, copper palm trees, and pink dolphins, and she had deeply admired Ali's kingdom of Ababwa with its sloping hills, and rocky cliffs, and monarch butterflies— but she realized now: she *loved* Agrabah. For all its flaws and problems, Agrabah was home.

"Sometimes you just have to see it from a different perspective," Ali said.

"It's them." Jasmine nodded toward the wedding-goers in the distance. "*They* are what make Agrabah beautiful. And they deserve a leader who knows that. I don't know why I believe it could be me, but I do."

"Because it should be. You have the strength, the mind, the courage."

"You think so?" she asked him.

"Does it matter what I think?"

Jasmine paused to study him. While she certainly cared very much what Ali thought about things, he was right; when it came to being a leader of Agrabah, that was something she had to decide and act upon herself. And this truly was the biggest gift her magic carpet adventure had given her: she now knew her desire to be a leader wasn't simply fanciful daydreaming. She could do it. She was capable of being the leader her people needed and deserved. Jasmine would do whatever it took to become just that.

A breeze wafted through the air. Loose strands of hair fluttered against her forehead. Ali reached out and tucked a strand behind her ear. Not unlike the boy she had met the other day in the market. Jasmine smiled.

"Look at that cute little monkey down there." Jasmine leaned over the magic carpet and pretended to point to something on the ground beneath them. "Is that Abu?"

"No, it couldn't be Abu." He followed her gaze and

then paused with a start. Looking at her, his cheeks grew red as he realized he'd been found out.

"So how many names do you have, Prince *Aladdin*?" she asked. "I knew it was you!"

"What?" he said quickly. "No!"

"Who is Prince Ali?"

"I am," he said. "I like to go among the people so I can learn more about those who I wish to govern."

Jasmine paused. They had, after all, spent their time in Ababwa out and about walking among his people, and they appeared to take it all as ordinary and uneventful for a prince to walk among them as casually as he did. Jasmine frowned. But that was different, wasn't it? That was his own kingdom of Ababwa.

"How could you know *this* city so well?" she asked him.

"I came to Agrabah early because if you want to know a people you have to see them for yourself. But you know this—when I met you, you were disguised in your own city."

"But . . ." Jasmine couldn't make sense of it. "How did I not recognize you?" She couldn't believe it. She'd spent an entire day with him, and though she'd suspected who he was, how could it have taken her this long to realize this *was* Aladdin, the same boy who had charmed her completely in the streets of Agrabah?

"People don't see the real you when you're royalty," Aladdin said.

He was right about that. She saw how differently people treated her when she was out in Agrabah cloaked in her handmaiden's clothing as compared to how they treated her when she was dressed in her full regalia. People saw only her title when they saw her as a princess.

"I'm embarrassed," she admitted. "You saw more of this city than I have in a lifetime."

Aladdin's gaze settled on her, and suddenly all she could think about was him. After a night full of travel and adventure, on this magic carpet floating above Agrabah together, Jasmine looked at Ali and felt the funniest sensation—as though her insides had turned to butter. The way he looked at her, his eyes so warm and brown . . . she could get lost in those eyes forever.

"We should probably get back," Aladdin said after a moment. "It's nearly morning."

"Is it?" Jasmine looked up at the sky and felt a stab of disappointment. The sun was indeed poking out from the horizon. She knew they had shared more time together than she could have ever hoped for, and yet as it drew to a close, she wanted more. Jasmine sighed as the magic carpet turned away from the festivities and began to fly toward the palace. Glancing at Aladdin's rueful expression, she knew he felt the same as she did.

The carpet gently helped Jasmine back onto her balcony. Aladdin hovered midair on the magic carpet just on the other side.

"See you later, Princess," Aladdin said. He hesitated. She saw the longing in his eyes. She felt it, too. No matter who he was, no matter whether his name was Ali or Aladdin, she knew only one thing at this moment—she had fallen in love with him.

And then, just like that, Aladdin floated up. Toward her. And before she could think or say another word, he kissed her. His lips against hers. Jasmine closed her eyes and kissed him back. This kiss was more beautiful than she could have ever imagined.

It was perfect.

Epilogue

The Legend of Abbas

THE LAND was as desolate as Sultan Waleed had heard. He frowned as he arrived upon the rocky shores of the abandoned lands that had once been Moribania. His people had reported that they could not find Abbas anywhere when they had last come to replenish his provisions. Perhaps he had had taken his life on the rocky cliffside of the abandoned lands, but as Sultan Waleed checked upon the extra wooden pallet of food and provisions they had left behind, he saw that it was empty.

Then the sultan heard a sound. It sounded like a parrot, squawking the same words over and over again in the distance.

"Your Majesty," a soldier said nervously, "we can send our men to see what is going on, but we urge you to stay back. It may not be safe."

"Let us go together," Waleed said somberly. Together they walked toward the noise—and then, through three columns of boulders resting against one another, they saw a light glowing and heard the sound grow louder.

As they approached, Sultan Waleed understood the sounds they heard earlier were not the squawks of a bird, but the maniacal laughter of a man—of Abbas. He sat by the glow of the fire and laughed and spoke in animated conversations to himself. The words were garbled, and Waleed could not make them out.

"Abbas," Waleed said quietly once he had approached the man.

Abbas jumped at the voice. He turned around. His eyes met Waleed's. They widened and then they narrowed.

"Another figment has arrived, has it?" He stumbled up to his feet and unsteadily drew near the sultan. Two soldiers moved to block his path.

"It's all right," Waleed told the men. "Let him approach."

Abbas walked until he was face to face with his former friend. He was a pale version of his old self. His hair thin and wispy, his face lined with cuts and scars and bruises.

"You're just as real as the last one," he finally said.

"Last one?"

"Yes." Abbas nodded vigorously. He reached out and touched the king's robe. The soldiers took a step forward, but Waleed gave a subtle headshake, telling them to stay back.

"The clothing and"—he glanced up at Waleed's cream-colored hat—"the hat, everything. All of it. Just like the other time. That other man. How do these sorcerers do it?"

"Has someone else come here?" Waleed asked him.

"Oh yes." Abbas nodded vigorously. "The man—he had a whole kingdom here. It was out of this world, I'll have you know. He built it from nothing! It started with a burst of gold and red and blue bursting into the sky. And then . . . you should've seen it! It was outrageous. Tall golden minarets and a ruby-encrusted roof. It was five stories high, it was. And he had a carpet. It was made of magic. I almost got it." His face reddened. "I almost got it."

"You saw this?" Waleed asked him.

"Yes!" Abbas shouted. "Are you unable to process common conversations since we last spoke? I saw it all. And then it vanished. It was a figment. Or maybe it was real." His expression grew confused. "It felt real. But it wasn't real. But you look real. Are you real?" He reached out and touched the sultan's shoulder.

Waleed looked at him quietly. His friend, the one who had grown up playing sports with him. Who had read books side by side with him and gone horseback riding with him through the verdant fields of Sulamandra. His friend had gone mad. Waleed looked around. In a desolate land like this, what else could one do but go mad? Yes, Abbas had betrayed him and caused much harm to his beloved kingdom—he had burned nearly half of it to the ground.

But did any man deserve this?

Without warning, Abbas rushed toward the king and shoved him with all his force. He had grown considerably frail, so the impact was minimal—but the soldiers now gripped Abbas's arms on either side while the man laughed hysterically.

"Still weak as ever, eh, Waleed?" Abbas cackled.

"Your Majesty." A soldier approached King Waleed. "I will stay here and watch him until you are securely back on the ship."

"He's coming back with us," Waleed said quietly.

"Sultan Waleed," the soldier said, hesitating, "forgive me for saying this, but he tried to attack you just now."

Waleed looked at Abbas. The years had not softened the man's heart. It seemed they had only hardened it further. And yet it was also self-evident, with the way he raved and ranted about a nonexistent prince and a magic rug and a kingdom that had appeared and disappeared, that the man was not well.

"However he behaves, that is upon him," Waleed finally said. "But how I choose to conduct myself, that is a reflection upon me. The man is ill. He deserves medical attention and care. He deserves mercy."

"Where am I going?" Abbas shouted as he struggled against the men.

"Sulamandra," the sultan said.

"S-S-Sulamandra." Abbas stopped struggling. He

turned toward the sultan. "You mean I can go home?"

Sultan Waleed nodded.

"Thank you." Abbas's eyes filled with tears.

And so the men brought Abbas onto the ship and covered him with a blanket, whereupon he collapsed on the ground and fell asleep surrounded by vigilant guards. As the gray seafaring ship began its return to Sulamandra, Sultan Waleed glanced back at the inky horizon where they had come from.

And then, he frowned.

For in the distance, upon the land they had just left, he could have sworn he saw a glimmer—a burst of gold and red and blue, a flicker of light glowing brighter and brighter—and then, just like that, it vanished. He squinted, but the land lay dark and still as it ever had. Sultan Waleed glanced down at the sleeping frame of his former friend, a curious expression upon his face.